SAVING CHRIS MOSS

CHRIS MOSS TALES BOOK ONE

BEA STEVENS

In Memory Of

Jane Wenham-Jones

1

———

'NICK SAINT? SERIOUSLY?'

Being stuck on a smelly, rickety old train on my way to goodness-knows-where isn't my idea of a fun Christmas. Neither is hurling myself and my baggage out of the carriage and landing face-down in the mercifully thick snow at Merryville Station.

'Need a hand?'

I'm still in a state of shock when I look up into the sparkling blue eyes of a handsome guy in a thick, red, woollen coat. His white-blond hair shines like a halo around him, making me gasp. He reaches down to help me up, and I gladly clasp his hand and haul myself to my feet. While I shake the snow off my very stylish, but now very wet, thick winter-white duffle coat, he starts gathering up the myriad bags I've just thrown, along with myself, onto the now-empty platform.

When I say empty, it's just not people it's devoid of, its... well... Christmas! Usually by now the whole building is festooned with multi-coloured, twinkling lights, as are the lamp-posts and all the planters, which are usually full of bright red and white poinsettias. A large tree usually greets visitors at the entrance, again bedecked with lights, huge baubles and lots of knitted ornaments that the local Women's Institute painstakingly adds to each year. Often, I hear carollers in the square just outside, and even our Town Crier makes the odd appearance to welcome tourists who pile off the train. Something else that seems to be missing this year. What's happened to Merryville? And, more importantly, what's happened to *Christmas*?

It's what had me stumped as soon as the train had drawn up, and the reason I'd been so busy gaping out the window that I'd almost forgotten to get off. It was only when people started piling on, that I realised I was going to end up somewhere in deepest, darkest Wales if I didn't make a move quickly. I felt like a salmon swimming upstream as I tried to squeeze through the crowd with my wheelie suitcase and my bags of gifts and goodies. After feeling the train jerk, I knew it was about to continue its journey with, or without, me, and that's when I'd flung myself towards the door in a last-ditch attempt to get off.

Understandably, everyone saw me coming and swiftly dodged out of the way, leaving me to plummet from the carriage and end up sprawled in the snow, looking more like a demented frog than a snow-angel.

'I think that's all of them,' the guy says, now laden with my bags. 'I'm Klaus, by the way.'

I have to take a few bags from him so we can shake hands, and I'm surprised to feel how warm his is. I'm also surprised that I didn't notice this earlier and can only surmise it was due to my state of shock. His long fingers curl around my shivering skin and, for a moment, I don't want to let go.

'Christina Moss,' I tell him. 'Thanks so much for your help.'

He seems a little surprised at my resistance, so I finally release his hostage hand and give him a big smile. Luckily, he reciprocates, making cute dimples appear on his rosy cheeks.

'Have you got far to go?' he asks, starting to steer me towards the exit – which, incidentally, is yet another disappointment in the decorations department.

'About a fifteen-minute ride,' I reply.

'I'm taking a taxi to the Hollies Hotel,' he says, as we head for the rank. 'Is that anywhere near where you're going?'

'Just up the road.'

'Great. Fancy sharing?'

I thought he'd never ask! 'Good idea.'

He helps load my luggage, along with his case, into

the boot of the taxi and we climb into the warm, back seat. The leather smells old, but not unpleasant, and I notice the driver's quietly playing Christmas Carols on the radio as we head out of town.

I don't recognise the driver, but then, I hardly recognise the town as we hum swiftly along. I've never seen it look so bare. There are no lights in the streets, no decorations in the windows of the houses as we pass by, and not even a snowman in any of the gardens. I've never known Merryville to look so miserable at this time of year.

'Do you live around here?' Klaus asks, as I lean into the soft seat, finally starting to warm up.

'Yes. Well... no. My parents do, and I used to, but I moved out a couple of years ago. I always come home for Christmas, though. How about you?' I ask, annoyed at myself for sounding so awkward. I still feel like a local, even though I now live in a tiny flat in Greenchurch.

'My dad's having a house built here,' he tells me. 'With an annexe for me in the grounds. It's a compromise; I like my independence but he wants me to take over the family firm so it makes sense for me to live here. I've been staying over in Higher Ludd where I work, but the house should be ready just after Christmas so I'll be moving back.'

'That sounds lovely. What do you do?'

'I've been working as a marketing manager but

finished the job this morning. The family owns Merryville Toys.'

My eyes widen. 'Wow, that's great. I've always loved it there.'

It's one of those shops with a real homely feel, where you can lose yourself in nostalgia as they sell all sorts of handmade, wooden toys that become heirlooms. Another part of the shop is dedicated to the latest 'must-haves' that kids look for these days.

'It's been in our family for generations,' Klaus says, proudly. 'Though my grandad's not too keen on the modern section. He'd have preferred to stick with the traditional toys, but Dad insisted we need to move with the times.' He shakes his head. 'It's been the subject of quite a few arguments, I can tell you, and it looks like I'm going to be stuck right in the middle of it.'

'Oh no.' I frown. That can't be nice.

'I can see it from both sides,' he goes on. 'But I've always been really close to my grandad so I can see him trying to get me to agree with his point of view.'

'What about your dad?'

'He's not as nostalgic. Sees it as a business, more than a family institution. Besides, Dad's got his own company just outside Merryville. He's a lawyer. He's not really interested in the shop.' Klaus grimaces.

'But I'd have thought it would be a lovely place to run, especially at Christmas,' I say, surprised. 'All those kids gazing at the toys, wondering what they'll find in their stocking on the big day. There must be so much excitement and fun in the place, surely your dad won't be able to resist getting caught up in the joy of it all?'

'Dad and I aren't all that big on Christmas, to be honest.'

My face falls, my jaw almost hitting the floor. 'Not big on Christmas?' I can't believe anyone could live in Merryville and not be excited about the festivities – it's what the whole town thrives on. Tourists come from miles to join in with our Christmas markets and to see the lights and decorations all around the quaint little town. Everyone makes an effort here, and it's impossible not to get swept up in the excitement of it all. I suppose that's why it's so disappointing to find that nothing seems to have been done yet to get the town ready. We're usually awash with tourists by now, and the Hollies Hotel is always bursting at the seams at this time of year.

I notice a sadness in Klaus's eyes and don't want to upset him by asking questions, so I change the subject.

'Is your grandad staying at the hotel, too?' I ask, trying to sound casual.

He smiles. 'Yeah. He and Grandma wouldn't miss Christmas with me and Dad. It's all part of the family tradition, especially since...' He stops himself and swallows hard.

I stare at him. He hasn't mentioned his mother. What if...?

'My mum died on Christmas Eve,' he explains, as though reading my thoughts.

I gasp, putting my hand to my mouth.

'It's okay. It was a long time ago. I was only ten. She was on her way home when a drunk driver crashed into her car.' He sighs. 'Since then Dad just hasn't been interested in Christmas. If it wasn't for my insistent grandparents I probably wouldn't have ever celebrated it again.'

'Oh Klaus, I'm so sorry. That's awful.'

'Like I said, it was a long time ago.'

'Even so...'

'It's fine, honestly.' He gives me a reassuring smile and places his warm hand on mine. 'Anyway, that's enough about me. Christina's a lovely name, are you called Chris for short?'

'How did you guess?' I grin at him, knowing what he must be thinking. 'I prefer Klaus Bytheway,' I say, getting in there before he makes a quip about my name.

He raises his perfectly-shaped black eyebrows in surprise.

'Sorry,' I say, a little sheepishly, 'I just couldn't resist.'

A massive grin practically splits his face in half. My stomach becomes jittery at the sight. He looks even more gorgeous when he smiles like that. He throws his head back and gives a laugh.

'Don't be,' he says, when he's recovered. 'It's not the first time anyone's joked about my name, but that's a new one.' He was still grinning.

I frown, puzzled. 'Usually it's *my* name that's being laughed at,' I admit.

'Chris Moss is brilliant,' he agrees with a nod.

'I'll take that as a compliment,' I reply with a smile. 'I just wish my school reports had said something more like that.'

He chuckles. 'I need to come clean,' he says. 'It's only fair.'

My good mood suddenly takes a nosedive. Is he about to say he's married? Engaged? Gay?

He rolls his eyes as though reading my thoughts again. 'My surname is Saint,' he says, almost conspiratorially.

My jaw drops. 'You're called Klaus Saint?'

He nods. 'My great-grandfather was German,' he explains. 'My grandfather was named after him, and I was named after them both.'

I let out a sigh. 'What a good job no one in your family was Spanish then.'

I was really thinking aloud and am surprised when he bursts out laughing again. 'Santa instead of Saint? I get it.'

My eyebrows rise in amazement. It's strange for anyone to 'get' my sense of humour.

'Mind you, it didn't stop me being called Santa

most of my life anyway,' he adds. 'But I suppose there are worse nicknames.'

I narrow my eyes, as my mind whirls. 'You said you were named after your grandad and great-grandad,' I say. 'What about your dad? Wasn't he a Klaus, too?'

He closes his eyes, shaking his head. 'You just had to go there, didn't you?' he says, opening his eyes again, which are now twinkling with mirth.

My eyes widen with realisation and I put my hands to my mouth. 'Oh no.'

'Yup.' He nods. 'I suppose I had a lucky escape. Dad's called Nicholas.'

'Nick Saint? Seriously?' Tears of joy pool in my eyes but I try hard not to show them in case he's offended.

'Been Saint Nick all his life,' Klaus says, shaking his head with a smirk.

'I'm sorry, but that is so funny.' I have to let out it out before I burst, and feel relieved when he laughs right along with me.

'It's good to know mine isn't the only family with a twisted sense of humour,' he says, wiping his eyes.

I shake my head. 'Oh no. Wait till you've met mine. You have no idea.'

'I'd love to,' he says, his voice suddenly much softer.

My stomach fizzes as I turn to look into his handsome face. Did I really just invite this gorgeous stranger to meet my parents?

WE REACH my house before his hotel, and I reluctantly slide out of the warm car into the cold evening air. Klaus is the perfect gentleman and gets out too, going round to help the driver retrieve all my bags from the boot.

'Can you manage?' Klaus asks, piling me up with my belongings.

'Yes, but I need to pay for my fare.' I suddenly realize that my handbag is now swung around my back, with another, heavier bag slung on my shoulder over it.

'I've got it,' Klaus assures me. 'I'd have to pay it anyway, but it's been much nicer to have your company for a while. I don't think I've laughed so much in ages.'

'Well, I'll pay for coffee or something,' I offer boldly. *Well it **is** the twenty-first century!*

'I'll look forward to it,' he says with a beaming smile. 'Just call me at the hotel; we can swap numbers next time.'

'Okay, great.' I'm not sure if he can see me smiling beneath all the bags and boxes I'm laden with, but I hear him get into the car, so I head up the pathway to my parents' large house.

It's sad to see that there are no lights around it, as is usual for this time of year. There are none of Dad's mechanical ornaments in the garden, nodding their heads, and even the big Santa who usually yells 'ho ho ho' to anything that moves hasn't made an appearance this year.

The neighbours always joke that our house is so brightly-lit at Christmas that it can be seen from space, but that's certainly not the case this year.

The snow is compacted beneath my feet and I find it hard not to slide up the path. I'm wearing sensibly flat-heeled boots, but I can't see where I'm going with all these bags and gifts, and I suddenly bump into something hard that must be the doorstep and find myself hurtling head first through the open door, for the second time today.

Mum's arms reach out and grab me just in time to save me falling face-first on the hallway carpet. My parcels and bags fly from my hands, freeing them to throw around Mum's neck. She's as steady as a rock as she envelopes me in a hug while I gasp, heart pounding, at my near-fall.

Mum doesn't bat an eyelid. 'Welcome home, love.'

2

'CHOCOLATE HOBNOBS? HAS SOMEONE DIED?'

It takes a few minutes for me to catch my breath, but Mum seems oblivious to my ordeal as she wraps me in a big hug.

'We were expecting you to call your dad from the station when you got in. You didn't need to waste money on a taxi, love.'

'I didn't. I got a taxi, but someone else paid for it. He was going to the hotel anyway.'

I'm surprised to see the relief on Mum's pretty face. Then I look around the hallway and am even more surprised to see not one piece of tinsel or holly hung anywhere.

'Is Dad okay?' Panic begins to rise in my stomach, replacing that warm, fuzzy feeling you get when you step into your old home for the first time in months, and are met by your Mum on the doorstep.

'He's fine, love.' She tucks one of her wayward brown curls behind her ear with a smile. 'He's just in the kitchen. Went to put the kettle on as soon as we heard a car.'

I smile. *Good old Dad!*

Mum closes the door as I head towards the kitchen and throw my arms around Dad. No one gives cuddles like my dad. In his arms is the only place where all my troubles truly melt away, just as they always have.

'Dad, what's going on?' I chance a look at his soft, warm face as I slowly pull myself from his embrace. He looks older than I remember, his dark hair has slightly more grey wisps around the edges, and he's a little tense around his jaw line.

'It's okay, love. Nothing crucial.' He sounds cheerful but his eyes tell a different story.

With a lump in my throat, I follow him into the lounge as he carries the tray of tea. I quickly peel off my coat and hang it in the hallway on my way through, and we join Mum by the fire.

'How are you?' Mum asks as I plonk myself on the big, soft, squidgy sofa.

'I'm fine, Mum. Honestly. I've been so looking forward to coming home to see you guys, especially with Christmas and everything. But...' I look around the room, which, again, has no sign of the festive season. 'What's happened?'

'We're not celebrating Christmas this year, love,' Mum explains with a sigh.

My stomach lurches. 'What?' I frown. We've never not celebrated Christmas. 'Why?'

Dad offers me a cup of a tea. When I spy the biscuits on the plate I know something's very wrong. The luxury of chocolate oatiness is only ever reserved for real crises like boyfriend breakups, poorly relatives —or worse.

'Chocolate Hobnobs? Has someone died?' The words spill out of my mouth, at the same time as some of my tea spills out of the mug and down my favourite Christmas jumper.

'No, love. Of course not.' Mum's quick to reply, and even quicker to offer me the box of man-size tissues from the shelf.

'The factory had to close,' Dad explains softly as I wipe tea from my clothes.

'What factory? *Your* factory?' My eyes widen with alarm.

Dad nods sadly. 'Jumpers for Joy. Some hotshot came in from goodness-knows-where and took all our business. They've opened another factory over at Showford. Jupiter Jumpers.' He sighs. 'I suppose it was only a matter of time.'

'But they can't do that! It's part of our heritage,' I protest.

It's one of the key attractions on our Town Tourist

Trail, and enables visitors to come and see how the jumpers are made, and to buy them at a knockdown price. It's always good for business, and encourages a loyal customer-base for years to come.

'Their stuff can't be as good quality as the ones you've been making,' Mum grumbles.

'But we've got thousands of customers on the mailing list. And what about the repeat orders from the shops? They rely on Jumpers for Joy all year round. They can't just close you down.' My voice has raised a few octaves in indignance, and I'm sure only bats can hear me now, but I don't care. This is all wrong.

'I'm afraid they already have, love,' Dad replies, soothingly.

'It's a big trading estate that opened up a few months ago,' Mum explains, shaking her head. 'Now everyone's wondering what's going to get shut down next. The whole town's on edge. They took the decision to cancel Christmas this year in case we can't afford to pay our bills afterwards.'

'But what about the tourists?' I protest. 'What will they think when they all come flocking here and find there's no Christmas?'

'The council made an announcement,' Mum explains. 'The hotel's still expecting a few guests who couldn't cancel their plans at the last minute, but apart from that, everyone knows not to come.'

'But it's our main income. We can't just cancel it!' I

feel my cheeks go red hot and my bottom lip starts to quiver. 'The whole town will die if we don't keep Christmas on track.' A stray tear tickles my cheek as it rolls down, followed by another, then another. I rub a hand across my face, but I can't stop the deluge once it starts.

'Oh, love, don't get upset.' Dad comes over and sits next to me on the sofa, wrapping me in a warm bear hug. 'It's only one year. Things will be different in twelve months' time, you'll see.'

I shake my head. 'It'll be different because no one will want to come here again, Dad,' I say, before a deep sniff. 'Once word gets round that Merryville is no longer the place to go for Christmas, we'll never get them to come back. We have to do something now. We can't just give up like this.'

Mum smacks her lips together. 'She's got a point there,' she says.

'But what can we do? The town can't afford the electric bill without the revenue from the tourists, and when they hear the place is closing down they won't want to come. All our taxes will shoot up again next year, just when we've all lost our jobs.' Dad sounds so mournful, I just hug him tighter.

'But what about all the shops that order their jumpers from us? What's happened to them? Surely the shops haven't shut down, too?' I sniff again – not very ladylike, I know, but hey, I'm upset.

'One of our directors went to work for Jupiter Jumpers. Took the customers with him,' Dad replies.

I frown. 'But he can't do that.'

'He did.'

'Has Jupiter Jumpers bought us out, then?' I've only ever worked there temporarily to help me fund my way through college, but I still feel an affinity to the place, especially as Dad's worked there most of my life, having progressed to managerial status a few years ago.

Dad shakes his head. 'No, love. They just opened up their own place so we had to close.'

I frown. I've watched enough episodes of 'Suits' to know a little about commercial law, and I'm sure that's illegal even in *this* country.

'It's horrid seeing the whole place without any lights or decorations,' I moan, suddenly feeling helpless. 'Couldn't we at least put the tree up?'

Mum raises her eyebrows. 'Well, we could, but we can't afford to put the lights on in case the electric bill's too much.'

'But there's plenty we can do without using electricity,' I remind her, cheering up a little. 'All the decorations can still go up, and the garden ornaments. We just won't switch anything on, that's all.'

Dad squeezes me a little tighter. 'Alright, love. You'll need to help me get them all down from the attic in the morning, but I see no reason we couldn't make the place look a bit more festive.'

IT's lovely to wake up in my own bed the following morning, and to see the snowflakes dancing outside my window. A fresh blanket of the white stuff has smothered the town in the night, turning it into the scene from the top of a Christmas cake.

The chilly air urges me to quickly get ready and I go downstairs to find Mum and Dad sitting at the kitchen table, having breakfast.

'You're up early,' Dad says in surprise. 'I thought you'd be having a lie in this morning.'

'I would have, but there's so much to do,' I remind him. 'We've got to get all the decorations up, and then I need to ring the hotel and see if Klaus wants to come out for a coffee. I thought we could go into town and see what's changed.'

Usually it's a delight to see the new shops that have opened up in Merryville, and to meet any new neighbours that have moved in since my last visit, but today feels different. Dread fills my stomach at the thought of what might have had to shut down, as a result of the new estate, and I'm afraid my home isn't going to be how I remember it at all. I never wanted to leave here in the first place, and if I'd known two years ago how horrid it would be working for a boring company, living in a boring flat in a boring town three times the size of Merryville, I would never have left.

Mum and Dad were so proud of me getting a job in advertising, though, and I don't want to disappoint them by telling them how much I hate it. It's not the job so much as the people. They're not half as friendly as those in Merryville, and everyone's always in such a rush for everything. There really isn't time to chat and get to know my colleagues, as there's always so much to do. I can't help thinking that if the management in that company were more organised we wouldn't all be running around like headless chickens the whole time, but I can hardly say anything, can I?

'Klaus?' Mum raises her eyebrows in surprise, while pouring me some tea. 'The old man who owns the toy shop?'

I gawp at her. 'You know him?' I sit next to Dad and take some warm toast from the rack on the table.

'Of course, love. His family have owned that place for years. Don't you remember, I used to take you there for the Santa's grotto every year when you were small?'

I do remember. I would have sworn that that was the only place I ever saw the *real* Father Christmas. As I grew up and saw the ones in the big stores outside of town, I always longed for the one that I used to visit every year at Merryville Toys. I'd often wondered if he was still there, but surmised that he was probably long gone. I suppose that's what stopped me from going back there after I grew up; it wouldn't be the same without that Santa. Besides, I didn't really have any reason to go to the toy shop once I'd outgrown all my toys.

'You're thinking of Klaus's grandad,' I inform her. 'His name's Klaus, too.' I finish my toast before leaning across the table for another slice. It's delicious.

'There's another one?' Dad asks, putting his newspaper to one side.

I nod. 'I met him last night. They're staying at the Hollies Hotel. That's who I got a lift back with, in the taxi.'

'He said his grandson was coming home at Christmas time,' Mum says with a smile. 'He's looking forward to having him back in Merryville to help with the shop.'

I frown. 'Please say the toy shop's all decorated for the big day?'

Mum purses her lips. 'I doubt it. That place has taken a hit with all the new stores opening up in Showford, too. Klaus senior is worried about the future of the business. They've been going for generations. It would be such a shame if they had to close down.'

A thud hits the pit of my stomach. I wonder if Klaus junior knows about the family struggle. He certainly didn't mention it yesterday. He'll be devastated if he's given up a good job in the city to come home only to find the family business is sinking.

'Are you ready to make a start?' Dad asks me, pulling me from my thoughts.

'Yeah. I'll just give Mum a hand with the dishes first,' I say, standing up to stack the plates.

'No, it's fine, love. You go with your Dad.' Mum glances from me to Dad. 'Actually, it might be best if *you* climb up into the loft. Your dad can hold the ladder.'

'No problem,' I reply, putting a pile of dishes next to the sink.

'I can go up and get everything down while she's helping you, dear,' Dad insists. 'Honestly, I'm not an invalid, you know.'

'You soon will be if you're not careful,' Mum fires back at him, firmly.

'It was nothing, dear. You worry too much.'

Now it's *my* turn to worry. 'What happened?'

'Nothing,' they both chorus at once.

'Tell me,' I insist, another uneasy feeling squeezing my stomach. I stare at them both, waiting expectantly.

'It was months ago,' Dad says, shrugging. 'And it didn't hurt that bad.'

'What didn't?'

'My ankle.'

'Did you break it?'

'No, of course not. Just twisted it when I landed on it, that's all. It swelled up a bit but your mother's a dab-hand with the frozen peas. Even the doctor was impressed when he came to check it out. Said she'd done exactly the right thing. It could have been a lot worse if she hadn't.'

I narrow my eyes at him. 'You fell onto your ankle? How?'

He frowns, a little unsure. 'Well, it was when I tumbled out of the attic. Goodness knows what happened to the ladder; it was there when I went up and I just assumed it was...'

'I was hoovering,' Mum interjects. 'I thought he'd finished up there and had forgotten to put the steps away. I moved it so I could do the landing.' She looks very sheepish.

I gape from one to the other. Now I'm *really* worried.

3

'OKAY, SANTA. SHOW ME YOUR BAUBLES!'

It takes a lot longer than I thought to fetch everything down from the loft and decorate the house, but it's well worth it when we've finished. There were only a couple of minor mishaps too—quite a record for our family. The first was when we put the tree up and it promptly fell over onto my head.

'Where there's no sense there's no feeling.' Dad had found it hilarious, and I was just pleased we'd opted for the artificial one this year to save spending money on a real one. I could only imagine pulling pine needles from my brown locks forever more.

Then Dad had gone out into the garden to arrange his mechanical menagerie, while I hung the garlands around the ceilings. How was I to know he'd decide to come back in while I was up the ladder, leaning over the front door to hang some fake mistletoe over it? *Well, you never know!*

'You need to be careful, love,' was his offering as I was hurled backwards through the air and leapt onto the stair behind me, catching the ladder before it could cause an injury. Dad has a way with words.

The phone rang while we were taking a well-earned rest, and tucking into a slightly late lunch of ham sandwiches with home-made pickle. I must live in the only house in England that still bothers with a landline, but Mum and Dad don't believe in mobile phones.

'It's the Hollies Hotel,' Mum says, turning back to me and Dad. My heart leaps until she offers Dad the receiver. 'Stanley needs some help with something.'

Dad gets up and takes the call.

'Your dad's been doing some odd jobs over there since the factory closed down.' Mum answers my unasked question, as she sits back at the table where I'm still finishing my cup of tea. 'Stan had a stomach operation a couple of months ago and he can't do any lifting or stand up for too long. It's given your dad something to do with his time.'

'But Dad's no spring chicken, Mum. Is he safe doing odd jobs over there? At least when he's here you can keep a close eye on him.'

'Oh yes. Margaret won't let him do anything too strenuous. Besides, I think she likes seeing Stanley have someone to talk to of his own age. And it's not as though your Dad's exactly busy nowadays, is it? I think it does them both good.' Mum finishes her tea and stacks up the cups.

I immediately get up and start on the washing up.

Dad's still on the phone to Stanley when I've finished, and they're not talking about odd jobs. Something to do with plastic modelling, I gather from Dad's side of the conversation. No wonder he's so keen to spend time with Stanley. It's always been a passion of Dad's since he was young, but he's never had time to do much while he was working. He's always said he'd take it up again when he retires. I only hope this set back with the factory isn't encouraging him to give up on work altogether; he's way too young to take early retirement and I don't think Mum could stand the thought of having him under her feet all day, every day.

'The place looks great, love.' Mum smiles as she comes back into the room.

'We need to get in the Christmas spirit,' I tell her. 'I don't care if there are no presents or fancy food or anything, but we've got to at least *feel* Christmassy.'

She nods. 'You're right. It's really cheered the place up, and I think we'll all feel a lot brighter for it, too.'

'I hope so, Mum.' I give her a big hug.

'Right, I'm off to the hotel,' Dad announces when he finally gets off the phone.

'Surely you can't have anything else to say to Stanley?' Mum shakes her head with a smile.

Dad gives a puzzled frown, then shrugs. 'He wants me to take a look at a leaking tap. I won't be long.'

'Can I come, Dad?' I release Mum from my arms and quickly smooth down my hair.

'You want to help me mend a tap?' Dad looks incredulous.

'No, I want to see if Klaus is free for that coffee.'

Mum and Dad exchange a knowing look.

'Do you want to come, too, Eve? I'm sure Margaret would love some company for a bit.' Dad raises his eyebrows to Mum.

'She's got a hotel full of guests. I'm sure she won't want me getting under her feet,' Mum replies.

'You can help her,' Dad suggests.

Mum purses her lips. 'I suppose it would be nice to have a bit of a chat and see if she needs anything.'

'Great. Get your coats, ladies, you've pulled.' Dad laughs.

'The only thing you're likely to pull is a muscle if you do too much around that place,' Mum replies with a shake of the head. 'Funny how you can do all that work at the hotel, but our shower still needs looking at.'

'I've told you. We need to get a man out for that one, dear.' Dad leads us through to the hallway and holds out Mum's coat for her to slip into. It's lovely to see how he still treats her like the lady she is.

THE SNOW GLISTENS in the afternoon sun as we make our way down the lane to the Hollies Hotel. It's a shame not to see the houses along the way all lit up as they usually are when I come home for Christmas, and an eerie quietness seems to have settled on the whole town.

As we near the hotel, although beautiful, it looks bare without the large tree that they always light up on the front lawn, and the myriad lights that, although are still strewn around the roof and windows, aren't switched on.

The car park, which is usually full of vehicles at this time of year, only has a couple there, including a rather odd-looking, large car with oversized tyres and a twin-exhaust.

'That's Comet, Klaus's car,' Dad explains, clearly noticing my bewildered expression. 'Klaus senior, that is. It's his pride and joy. The only car I've ever heard of with a souped-up engine that doesn't make a huge racket when it starts up. He's done all sorts of modifications to it so it'll go faster.' He giggles. 'He reckons it practically flies.'

I smile. It's nice that the old man has a hobby to keep him occupied.

As we let ourselves into the small reception area, we all stand still and stare. Decorations are everywhere. Although, like ours, there's not a twinkling light in sight. Furthermore, Slade's 'Merry Xmas Everybody is blaring out of the old jukebox in the bar, which, by the sound of it, is full of people.

'I thought you said they weren't doing Christmas this year.' Mum looks accusingly at Dad.

'That's what Stanley said. Same as the rest of us.' Dad looks bemused as we go into the packed bar.

A huge, decorated artificial tree stands in the corner near the fire, and garlands are hanging from the ceiling. Klaus is up a ladder, fixing a large star ornament above the mirror at the back of the room, and he grins at my reflection when he sees us arrive.

Even without the lights, the atmosphere is warm and welcoming, and I can't help beaming at him.

'The young lad there insisted we decorate the place up,' Stanley tells Dad, nodding at the handsome guy who's just climbing down the ladder. 'I wasn't going to bother but he insisted. I said I had no objection as long as he didn't mind helping. He's been an absolute whizz.'

'Funnily enough, someone else here had the same idea,' Dad replies, gesturing to me with a jerk of his head.

'Not that we're complaining,' Mum pipes up, smiling. 'You can't help feeling better with all this colour and glitter around, can you?' She lightly strokes a garland of pink and white tinsel that's been fastened to the front of the bar.

'That's just what I said, Eve.' Margaret suddenly appears behind us with a big grin on her face and a plate full of hot sausage rolls in her hands. 'Anyone hungry?'

No one needs asking twice, and we all delve in, as Klaus comes over, wearing a bright green jumper with a jolly-looking snowman on the front.

'Could you pass these round for me, Klaus?' Margaret offers him the tray, which he takes, gladly, before she and Mum find their seats over by the fire.

Dad's already chatting with Stanley over the bar, so I take full advantage of the opportunity to join Klaus and the food.

'Come and meet everyone,' he says, still grinning.

The bar is full of people, whom I presume must all be staying here. A couple of young boys are running around with plastic aeroplanes, making the engine noises as they swoop their toys through the air, one of them narrowly missing my eye on his way past.

There are other children playing the old board games Stanley and Margaret always have on hand, while adults are sitting around drinking and chatting, and a crowd of older kids congregate around the pool table. The atmosphere's electric and I can't help smiling, thinking how this is just as it should be on the run up to Christmas.

'This is my grandma, Anya,' Klaus tells me as we near an elderly lady sitting in an armchair by the window.

She offers me a beaming smile. Her hair is snow-white and as fluffy as a cloud, framing her pretty, round, red face, and her eyes sparkle like the stars on a frosty night. 'You must be Christina,' she says with a knowing look.

'Yes. It's lovely to meet you.' I can't help smiling back at her. She looks so happy and excited, sitting with a large crocheted blanket on her knees, her bright red jumper matching her cheeks.

'Klaus has told us all about you.' She gives me a wink, and I can't help wondering just what has been said.

'And this is Grandad.' Klaus waves his hand, gesturing to someone in a large armchair opposite, who has his face buried in a newspaper. 'Gramps, this is Chris.'

My jaw practically hits the floor when he moves the paper and looks up at me, smiling. It's him. Santa Claus. *The* Santa Claus. The one from the toy shop all those years ago. But it can't be – he must be over a hundred by now, surely? But it *is* him. Definitely. He's got the same bright blue twinkling eyes, and that smile under his soft moustache that I always longed to reach out and stroke, along with his downy white beard.

'Mary, how nice to see you again.' His voice is as booming as I remember, with that slight accent, and when he reaches out his hand to shake mine, I recognise those big, warm palms. It really is him. He's *here*. I also recognise the words he used to say to me every year when I went to see him in his grotto. Does this mean he actually remembers me?

'Mary?' Klaus frowns. 'Her name's Chris.'

'As if I wouldn't know a name.' His grandfather rolls his eyes, with a secretive smile.

'My first name *is* actually Mary,' I explain. 'My *middle* name's Christina, as is my mum's. I prefer it.'

Klaus's eyes widen and his face splits into a massive grin. He puts his hand to his mouth. 'Mary Christina Moss? Mary Chris Moss! This just gets better and better!'

'Look who's talking!' I exclaim. 'It was actually my grandmother's name. Though she didn't like it much, either.'

Klaus bursts out laughing, but his grandad just shakes his head.

'How are you?' I ask, suddenly remembering my manners.

'Very well, thank you. Very well indeed,' the elderly man says with a smile. 'Better now we've got the place looking a bit more like it. What d'you think?' He waves a hand, gesturing the decorations surrounding us.

'It's beautiful.' I reply with a smile. It really is, and it's so good to see how happy everyone seems to be because of it. It must be really miserable to come away for Christmas only to find the hotel you're staying at isn't making any effort for the festive season. In fact, it's unheard of in Merryville.

'It'll be even better once we've got all the lights on,' he says in a lower voice, putting his finger to the side of his nose with a wink.

My stomach does somersaults. How can he be so certain? Surely Margaret and Stanley must be as worried as the rest of the town about the bills piling in after the big day? Something in his smile gives me confidence, though, and for the first time since I returned home I actually believe that everything really is going to be okay.

'There's an even bigger tree to go up in the foyer,' Klaus informs me, when he's quite finished his fit of hysterics. 'Fancy giving me a hand with it?'

His eyes are so warm as he smiles at me, I can't help but feel drawn to him.

'If you can refrain from laughing at me for long enough,' I jibe.

His face falls. 'I wasn't laughing at *you*,' he assures me. 'It's just...'

'My name, I know.'

He takes my hand. 'Tell me I didn't offend you?' He actually looks quite contrite and my heart goes out to him.

I grin. 'Of course not, I'm just kidding.'

His eyes widen. '*You!* I really thought I'd upset you then.'

'As if!'

'I'd never want to do that, honestly,' he says, shaking his head. I can see by his serious expression he really means it, and suddenly feel mean for joking like that.

'It's fine. Come on – let's see if this tree's as impressive as you make out.'

We both laugh as he leads me back out of the bar and into the foyer, still holding my hand.

Stanley's already put the large, eight foot tall artificial tree in the foyer while I was meeting Klaus's family. Norwegian Spruce, its branches bow majestically towards its crown. The needles are velvety to the touch, and it looks so beautiful it almost seems a shame to decorate it.

'Oh wow!' Klaus's eyes light up as he notices the boxes of decorations that have been stacked on the floor by the reception desk, and he leads me over to them.

They are a riot of colour, which is just what the place needs. He drops my hand to delve into one of the boxes.

'How did you convince Stanley and Margaret to let you decorate the place?' I ask, giggling as he throws a length of silver tinsel around my neck.

'I can be very persuasive when I want to be.' He winks, pulling me towards him by gently tugging each end of the tinsel.

I grin, as my stomach does an impressive number of cartwheels—more than I could ever do, that's for sure. He smells clean and fresh, and his whole body feels ripped as I get close enough, and grab his biceps to steady myself.

'I think you need some of this, too,' I tell him, reaching behind him to pull some red tinsel from the box. 'Hmm, that really is your colour.' I mean it, too; he looks great in red.

He narrows his eyes at me, a little suspiciously. 'You're not going to say it matches my bloodshot eyes, or something, are you?'

I gape at him. 'No, I was not.'

He doesn't look convinced, so I continue. 'You're eyes aren't in the least bit red. They're blue like...' I swallow hard, realising how close I am to him, and that I'm gazing into his deep, sparkling eyes. 'Sapphires.'

His lips curl in a sweet smile and my heart melts at the sight. 'And yours are big and brown like...'

My breath hitches as he stares back into my face. My skin feels like goose-flesh and heat rises in my cheeks. I can't help thinking how lovely this guy is, and it's hard to believe we only met yesterday. I feel like I've known him for years.

A movement behind him catches my attention, and I let out the breath I've been holding. 'Shit.' I quickly take a step backwards.

Klaus frowns incredulously. 'I wasn't about to say *that*,' he assures me. 'I was thinking more of—'

'Ahem.' I clear my throat, jerking my head to indicate the man standing behind him.

Klaus turns around and rolls his eyes.

'Don't let me stop you, son. I only came out to see if you two wanted some hot chocolate.' He holds up two steaming mugs, grinning.

'Thanks, Dad. This is Chris.' Klaus seems totally unperturbed as he reaches over, takes the drinks from him and places them on the reception desk in front of us.

Looking at the guy properly I can certainly see the resemblance. His hair is almost white-blond, and he has the same blue twinkling eyes that seem to run in the Saint family.

The heat in my face only increases as he smiles at me, and I wonder how long he's been standing there.

'Hi, Chris. I'm Nick.'

'It's nice to meet you,' I reply with a shy smile.

He looks around the foyer. 'You're working your magic out here too, then?' He gives his son an incredulous look.

'Yes, Dad. I think everyone needs cheering up a bit, and this is the best way to do it. Besides, there are young kids staying here, and it's only fair for them to have a happy Christmas.'

Nick says nothing, just nods and heads back towards the bar.

'Is he okay with all this?' I ask, once he's out of earshot. 'I mean, he's not offended or anything, is he?'

Klaus shakes his head with a grin. 'He's fine. He totally gets that other people want to celebrate the season, even if *he's* not so keen. Honestly, don't worry about him. Let's get this tree looking as festive as we can.' He waves one end of his tinsel in the air, to make his point.

I giggle, winking at him. 'Okay, Santa. Show me your baubles!'

4

'THAT TREE NEEDS A STAR'

The tree is set in a large, ornate, metal stand just near the main door. I can't help thinking what a lovely welcoming sign it will give to visitors, and I'm so glad Klaus managed to convince Margaret and Stanley that it would be a good idea to put it up, and to decorate the place, after all.

'We need to put the lights on first,' Klaus insists, pulling a box from the assortment on the floor.

I raise my eyebrows. 'But we can't switch them on this year,' I remind him. 'So what's the point?'

Klaus grins, shaking his head. 'You never know.' He has the same secretive smile as his grandad; the sort that fills you with hope.

He looks so confident, I decide not to argue, and pull the step-ladder over from the corner behind the reception desk.

'Hey, I'll do that,' he says, quickly coming over to help. I've never known anyone so chivalrous—apart from my dad, of course—so I stand back and allow him to lift it over to the tree and set it up. 'Hand me the lights,' he says, climbing up the steps.

I do as he asks, watching as he skilfully winds the flex up and down the branches in perfectly-even loops. He starts and finishes at the top of the tree, with the last light bulb settling on the topmost branch. I can't believe how he's managed to calculate it so precisely, but it looks totally flawless.

'How did you do that?' I ask, staring at his workmanship. He did it all so quickly and elegantly, not once having to go back and re-do a bit, like I would have.

'You don't get a name like Santa without knowing a few things about Christmas,' he says, smiling. He nods at his handiwork. 'Tinsel next.'

He clearly has a system for all this, and I'm not about to argue. It actually takes me and Dad a good couple of days to get the tree right at our place, and it's not even half as big as this beauty. It's a shame we're all using artificial trees this year, but I can see that it saves money, and, anyway, once it's decorated no one will notice the difference. Apart from the smell, of course. There's nothing like the 'green' smell of a fresh tree. Mind you, there's nothing like the pine needles, either, that shed everywhere, and turn up still lurking in shady corners at Easter. I won't miss the sound of the hoover every morning as Mum fights to keep up with the darn things, that's for sure. I'm guessing Margaret feels the same way – it's a bit like painting the Forth Bridge.

Something tickles the side of my neck and I jump.

'You looked miles away,' Klaus says, wrapping a thick length of green tinsel around my neck like a scarf. It's quite warm with two layers of tinsel, but I'm glad of it, standing by the draughty front door.

'I was just thinking,' I tell him, stopping myself before I admit that I was actually admiring how adept he is at all this.

'Well, our hot chocolate's going cold,' he says, bringing over the cups from the reception desk.

I take a sip, relieved that it's still warm. It really is delicious, and Margaret's even floated tiny marshmallows on the top, which have all but melted by now. Someone in the bar has started the old juke box up again and Mariah Carey serenades us as we finish our drinks before picking out strands of tinsel and lametta for the tree.

With songs playing in the background, we have a great time adorning not only the tree, but every picture, lampshade, and surface in the foyer.

'Time to put the star on top of the tree,' Klaus announces, pulling it from one of the boxes. 'Do you want to do the honours?'

'I'd love to.' I position the steps in front of the spruce once again and climb up, a little tentatively.

As I turn to take the star from him, one of the branches gets caught in the holes of my loose-knit jumper and I feel the weight of the whole tree sway towards me.

'Look out!' Klaus makes a grab for the thick trunk, swinging it back into position, but it pulls me with it, as I'm still attached to the branch.

'Aah!' I scream as I feel my feet being lifted from the stepladder, and for a moment I think I'm going to fly. Instead, my jumper suddenly frees itself and I plummet off the top of the steps and hurtle towards Klaus, whose bemused expression isn't half as horrified as mine, I'm sure.

My fear that I'll knock him over, and take the tree down with us, is mercifully unfounded, as he reaches out his arms and catches me, saving my dignity and, probably, a broken leg to boot. I'm suddenly in his embrace, and he lets me down gently, until I can put both feet on the floor without crumpling into a heap. I had no idea he was so strong, and his confident smile sends electricity humming through my veins. My body is so close to his, and his delicious scent envelopes me in a safe cloud of assurance and care as I stand, shaking in his arms.

'Are you okay?' His voice is soft and full of concern as he studies my face.

I'm still panting for air, not sure if it's the fall or his proximity that's made me so breathless, and set my heart thumping. Looking up into his deep blue eyes I find myself nodding, unable to speak right then.

He smiles, confidence oozing from his every pore, and I can't believe I ever thought he'd let me fall. Never once did he flinch, or step back, or give me any indication he'd let anything bad happen to me, and I couldn't be more grateful.

'We're about to eat,' a voice announces from the doorway, and it takes all my effort to tear my eyes from Klaus's.

'We'll be right there, Dad.' He looks up but doesn't let go of me. 'We just need to do a quick tidy up here first.'

'It's looking good.' His Dad nods, approvingly, before disappearing back into the bar.

'Are you sure you're all right?' Klaus turns his gaze back to me.

'Yeah,' I manage. 'I think so.'

'You just sit there a minute,' he says, gesturing to the set of steps. 'I'll sort this lot out and we can go and join the others.'

Dumbly, I do as he says, not having the energy to object. I watch as he deftly scoops up the boxes, tidying one inside the other before piling them neatly behind the reception desk. He hangs a few stray lengths of tinsel around the edge of the desk, then comes back over to me.

'Ready?'

I nod, standing up.

'I'll just... er...' He reaches behind me to fold up the steps and I'm treated to another waft of his clean scent as he does so.

As soon as he's stowed the stepladder in the corner, he smiles back at me. 'Dad's right,' he says, with a nod. 'It does look good.'

I follow his line of sight around the foyer and have to agree.

'That tree needs a star,' I point out with a grimace. I'm not even sure what happened to it after my little incident. One minute it was in my hand and the next it was gone, possibly broken into a million pieces behind the tree for all I know.

'It'll get one,' Klaus says calmly, with another of those knowing smiles.

I've learned better now than to ask questions, and, besides, I'm starving.

EVERYONE IS SAT around the little tables in the bar, eating hot food and chatting happily when we join them.

'Is beef stew and dumplings okay?' Margaret asks,

smiling as soon as she sees us. 'It's not very festive, I know, but it's warm and tasty.'

'Perfect,' I reply with a smile, as Klaus leads me over to where our parents have pushed several tables together and are just being served their food.

'There you are,' Mum says, smiling. 'Have you had fun?'

I nod. 'Yeah, we've just been decorating the foyer.'

Klaus pulls up a couple of chairs and I sit next Mum, with him next to me and his grandad to his left.

'Will the rest of the town mind all these decorations when they've agreed not to celebrate Christmas?' Nick asks as he tucks into his food.

My stomach lurches. I hadn't even considered that.

'Of course not,' Stanley assures him, putting a plate of piping hot stew in front of me. 'Why would they? It's not as if we've boycotted the big day; just not making a big fuss this year, that's all. Save everyone some money.'

Margaret arrives with the last of the meals and she and Stanley join us, sitting opposite Klaus and me.

'They'll all be decorating the place soon, you'll see,' Klaus announces, confidently.

'You reckon?' His dad doesn't seem so sure.

'Yeah. Once they see how nice this place looks they'll all follow suit.' He sounds quite matter-of-fact as he shrugs and then starts on his own meal.

'I still think we need to look into what's happened,'

I say, shaking my head. 'It can't be allowed. It's ruining everything for the whole town.'

Nick frowns, looking over at Dad. 'This is the closure of your factory?' he clarifies, his jaw tensing.

Dad nods. 'Not *my* factory, exactly; I'm just one of the managers.'

'The best one they've got,' Mum interjects, defensively.

'*Had,*' Dad corrects her.

'One of the managers defected to the new company and took the clients with him,' I explain, looking over at Nick. 'But they're not allowed to do that, are they? I mean, the clients belong to the *company*, not the manager—isn't that right?'

Nick narrows his eyes in thought. 'Does this manager own the company you worked for?' he asks Dad.

Dad shakes his head. 'Nope. Jumpers for Joy has several owners, but he's not one of them.'

'And where are these owners?' Nick enquires.

'Abroad,' Dad replies, gloomily. 'They're a family, The Hudsons, but they don't live in England. They're in Spain, I believe. The place is run by our management team. Or, at least, it *was*.'

'Do they know what's happened?' Klaus's grandad pipes up.

Dad nods. 'Yeah. One of my colleagues had the job of telling them. Unfortunately, the matriarch of the family, Stella Hudson, is very ill, and they don't want to leave her so they gave us the job of sorting it out. It was the senior manager who decided we were going to have to close to save running at a loss.' He smacks his lips together. 'Poor show all round, really.'

'What about the staff? Did they get redundancy pay?' Nick leans forward with interest.

'That's the saddest part,' Dad replies. 'No one got anything. It's down to the Hudsons to liquidise the firm. Without those orders there's not enough money to pay everyone, so they all got their final week's wages and were told to wait to hear from the family about the rest.'

'Right on Christmas? They can't do that!' I exclaim.

'They can't do that at *any* time of year,' Nick replies, shaking his head. 'Unless they've had the formal notification and the pay they're due, those staff are all still employees of the company.'

'So they should get paid from the time they stopped working until they get the redundancy pay sorted out?' I say, my mind working overtime.

Nick raises his eyebrows at me. 'That's right.'

'So no one's lost their jobs?' I clarify.

Dad sighs. 'The family wanted to make up their own minds about the future of the place, but it's just such a difficult time for them right now.'

'It's a difficult time for everyone,' I point out, defensively. '*And* it's Christmas.'

'We tried to tell Bob Robinson it wasn't fair, but his hands were tied by the Hudsons.' Dad looks even more miserable and my heart goes out to him. He must feel like he's being interrogated, but that's not the case at all.

'Who's the manager that's gone rogue?' Nick asks, before taking a sip of his wine.

'Gone rogue. I suppose I hadn't thought of it like that.' Dad raises his eyebrows.

'Rats desert a sinking ship,' Mum mutters.

'It wasn't sinking until he did this,' I remind her. 'The place was thriving.'

'That's the whole point,' Nick says.

'Drew Chapman,' Dad says. 'Always was a bit shifty, if you ask me. Though no one ever imagined he'd pull a stunt like this.'

'I don't know the name,' Nick admits, 'but I'll see if any of my associates do. See if there's any dirt we can dig up on the guy. Even if he's not done anything like this before, it doesn't make it right. He can still be sued for it.'

'What good would that do?' Dad asks.

'Probably not much from where you're stood,' Nick admits. 'But at least he'll get his comeuppance.'

I frown. 'But what about all the workers? And all our regular clients?'

Nick grimaces. 'Those customers had the right to go elsewhere if they wanted. We can't *make* them go back and give Jumpers for Joy their business if they don't want to.'

'But why would they? I mean, they've been loyal to that company for years.' I frown again.

'We can only assume they got a better offer. These big companies can afford to take a cut if they need to, in order to secure new business. They'll have made them an offer they couldn't refuse, I daresay. And we would never have been able to match it, being just a family-run business. 'Dad shakes his head.

'We should never assume anything,' I reply. *I'm sure I heard that on one of those legal programmes.* 'And anyway, shouldn't they have given us the courtesy of *asking* if we could match their offer?'

'You're right,' Nick says, looking impressed.

I don't get that very often, so I savour the moment. In fact, I've been savouring quite a lot of them recently, for various reasons.

'But they're not obliged to do so,' he goes on. 'And, I know it sounds harsh, but they probably guessed that a little family business wouldn't be able to match the offers of the big boys. Anyway, it's all supposition and unless someone can find out exactly what this other company's offer was we'll never know if the Hudsons could afford to do any better. But that's a big ask.'

'But not impossible.' I narrow my eyes at him, my brain whirling. *It does that a lot, actually.*

Nick offers me a quizzical look. 'Do you have something in mind?'

'Maybe.' Okay, so once I think of something I'll have it in mind. Until then I just have to come up with a brilliant idea – how hard can it be?

5

'...A BIT LIKE PULLING TEETH, APPARENTLY; LOTS OF EFFORT

—BUT PRODUCES NOTHING BUT HOLES.'

I'm up surprisingly early the following morning. It was quite late when we got home last night, but my mind was buzzing with ideas all night, and I'm not sure I got much sleep at all. Even so, I want to get on with my 'mission', as I've decided to call it.

'Operation Saving Christmas' is a two-pronged affair, I've realised. Not only do we need to convince the locals to reinstate the most magical time of the year, but we also have to find out what exactly happened at Jumpers for Joy and put it right. It's a bit of a chicken-and-egg situation really, as I'm sure if we could get back the jobs that have been allegedly lost at the factory, the mood of the whole town would lift anyway, and everyone will be only too happy to start celebrating again. Conversely, if we could re-book all the Christmas events and markets, and convince the council to put up the lights around the town we might still be able to attract tourists, who are always willing to spend their hard-earned cash on gifts and trinkets that can only be found in Merryville.

'Did you wet the bed?' Dad jibes, when I arrive in the kitchen. 'I wasn't expecting to see anything of you until at least noon.'

'I've got a busy day ahead,' I inform him, pouring myself a cuppa from the large teapot on the breakfast table.

Mum brings me over a clean plate. 'What're you up to?' she asks.

I narrow my eyes at her. She's always used this phrase when enquiring about my plans, and I'm sure it's her suspicious nature coming to the fore. Not that she's ever had anything to be suspicious of, of course. Well, not much, anyway.

'I'm going to save Christmas,' I announce, reaching for some toast.

That makes Dad put down his newspaper. Mum just gapes at me before they both exchange one of those looks that just screams of disbelief.

'Are you now?' Dad picks up his cup, suddenly taking an interest in his breakfast again.

'Yep. Starting with the toy shop, I think. Does Klaus's dad have much to do with it?'

Mum shakes her head. 'You'd think, wouldn't you?

No, he's not really interested in the place except from a business point of view. He's got a manager running it for him. He's in overall charge though, and makes all the big decisions, but he's got his own company to run. I can't see him ever giving up his lawyer's position to run that shop, despite it being in the family for generations. Shame, really.'

That explains why I didn't recognise him. Klaus's grandad was the store's Santa for years when I was growing up, and I'm pretty sure his grandma used to work behind the counter when she was younger, but I don't think I've ever seen Nick before.

'Klaus is going to take it on,' I announce, before crunching into my toast.

'Really?' Mum frowns. 'I wouldn't have thought it was the sort of career a young man would want.'

'He's qualified in business and marketing,' I tell her. 'He's ideal for that job.'

'Well, good luck to him,' Dad says. 'He seems a real go-getter, and, according to Stanley, could charm the birds from the trees.'

I smile, remembering how Klaus had managed to persuade Stanley and Margaret to let him decorate the hotel, which, I might add, was a brilliant idea. Looking around the kitchen, I'm glad Dad and I decorated here, too. There's nothing like a bit of tinsel and a few sparkles to get you into the Christmas spirit.

I frown, thinking about the second part of my

mission. 'So, how did the factory come to close without any official notice?' I ask Dad.

He clears his throat, and I hope I haven't just ruined the pleasant atmosphere.

'It was all a bit strange, really, love,' he says, shaking his head. 'We sent an order over to Poulson's Pullovers over in Craven Head but the driver was turned away. They said they already had their delivery earlier that day. It turned out that Jupiter Jumpers had fulfilled the order and told their staff that they would be supplied by them in future. We had no idea what had happened until Bob Robinson rang Jupiter's to ask what was going on, and then Drew informed him that they were now supplying Poulson's as well as all our other big clients. Talk about cheek.' He tightens his lips in annoyance.

'Of course, we double-checked and they had all signed their orders over to Jupiter's. We were left with all their orders and no one to sell them to, thanks to those fat cats.'

'Did anyone talk to the other companies to find out why?' I ask, frowning.

'One of the managers tried to, but everyone was very vague about it all. A bit like pulling teeth, apparently; lots of effort but produces nothing but holes. We were certainly none the wiser. It was all very strange, if you ask me. Anyway, we tried to sell the stock elsewhere, but only had a little luck—it seemed Jupiter's had got there first, no matter where we tried—and I can tell you, we had plenty of companies on our books.' Dad sighs, and I can see the toll all this has taken on him.

'They had no choice but to close the place down,' Mum pipes up, rubbing her hand over Dad's. 'They had loads of stock and no one to supply it to. And, as most of it was Christmas jumpers they knew it would be no good after the big day.'

'So why not keep trying? It's still nearly a fortnight to Christmas,' I point out. 'Surely someone should be out there now trying to sell it before it's too late?' I can't believe they've given up so soon.

'The marketing department tried, but said it was a waste of time. Jupiter's had swamped the market.' Dad looks really sad.

'*Stolen* the market, you mean,' I insist. 'They can't be allowed to do that. Surely these companies had signed contracts with your firm? How could they afford to pay the fines to be released?'

Dad shrugs. 'I've no idea.'

'Something's not right.' I know I'm only stating the obvious, but I can't help thinking aloud. 'Poulson's Pullovers was your biggest client wasn't it, Dad?'

He nods. 'Yeah. And the first to pull out on us. I never thought they would after all the years we've been working together, but I suppose it's business. I couldn't help feeling a little hurt that Frank Poulson didn't speak to us about it, though. I always thought we had a great relationship with him. A personal friend of the family, to my mind. It just goes to show how wrong you can be about people.'

'His wife babysat me a few times when I was little,' I remember.

'Fiona was a good friend of mine—or so I thought.' Mum looks wistful. 'One of those people you didn't see all the time, but when you did it was like you just picked up where you left off, you know? It was a shame they moved all the way out to Craven Head; we used to see each other all the time when they lived in Merryville.'

I can't help feeling sorry for Mum and Dad, as I finish my cup of tea and clear the table. After helping Mum with the dishes I pop back upstairs and pull one of my old Christmas jumpers from the bottom drawer of my dresser. I've got quite a collection, and this one's blue with a snowflake pattern all over it. Mum's going to see if the one I wore yesterday can be mended or not, but I'm not holding my breath, to be honest.

There must have been some frost in the night, as my boots crunch on the snow as I make my way over to the Hollies Hotel, and I pull my coat a bit tighter. I can't wait to see Klaus today – he hasn't been far from my mind all night and I hope he's up for helping with my mission.

The front lawn of the hotel has been decorated with a large, plastic Santa and Snowman, and yards of tinsel looped around the fence, and adorning the branches and trunk of the oak tree. Garlands of plastic holly hang over the front door, and even the pots of plants have been treated to some lametta.

'This looks lovely,' I gush as soon as I step inside and see Margaret behind the reception desk, typing something into her computer.

She beams. 'Young Klaus did it all this morning. And that was the third booking I've made so far today. It seems people are keen to visit Merryville despite being told we've cancelled Christmas this year.'

'Well, that settles it, then,' I say, as hope swells in my heart once more. 'We just *have* to have Christmas.'

Margaret raises her eyebrows. 'Good luck with that. Klaus Senior is very disappointed that the German Market's been cancelled this year.'

I swallow hard. It hadn't occurred to me that Merryville's longest-standing tradition would suffer the same fate as the rest of the festivities. It's such a lucrative event, bringing visitors from miles around to join in the fun.

'We need to save it.' I announce. 'Who's in charge of organising it?'

'Funnily enough, young Klaus was asking the same

thing earlier. It's Denise Blackenbury on the local council. He's gone over to the Town Hall to speak to her about it.'

I immediately do an about-turn. 'Right, I'll go join him.'

The local taxi company's number is still in my phone, and a driver comes out straight away. Merryville isn't a very large town, and it doesn't take me long to arrive at the large grey-stone building. Although quite pretty, with all the snow on the Georgian windowsills and slate roof-tiles, I can't help thinking it's a little bleak without the usual decorations we're used to seeing.

I stamp the snow off my boots before venturing inside, grateful for the warmth that greets me. *It looks like the town council aren't as worried about electric bills as the rest of the town.*

'I'd like to speak with Mrs. Blackenbury please,' I tell the receptionist with a sweet smile.

'Is she expecting you?' The grey-haired woman doesn't even look up from the keyboard she's tapping away at.

'No, but it's really important.'

'She's got someone with her right now.' She couldn't sound less interested.

'I know. I'm supposed to be in the meeting with them.'

She deigns a glance up at me, frowning. 'I thought you said you didn't have an appointment?'

'I'm with Klaus Saint,' I clarify. 'He's the one with the...' I trail off, not sure how Klaus managed to get past this Rottweiler without a written invitation from the councillor herself, but he seems to have a knack of getting around people. It doesn't matter, anyhow, as the receptionist seems to have already lost what little interest she may have perceived.

'They're in there.' She points vaguely towards the corridor opposite her desk.

'Thanks.'

Wasting no time, I head in the direction she's gestured and knock at the first door I come to.

At first there's no answer, but then the door opens and Klaus smiles at me. 'I wondered how long you'd be.' His eyes twinkle with mischief and I can't help wondering what I've missed.

'Sorry, I didn't mean to—'I'm stopped in my tracks when I see the room full of people, all sitting around a conference table.

I recognise Mrs. Blackenbury, still wearing those cat's eyes-shaped glasses she always had, sitting at the end of the table, seemingly holding court with her peers, who all seem to be over sixty with more hair growing from their noses and ears than their heads—*and that's just the women!*

'Come and sit down,' Klaus offers, leading me over to an empty chair next to his at the foot of the table.

'We were just discussing how important it is to keep the morale of the townsfolk by not cancelling the German Christmas Market,' Klaus explains.

I gape at him, slowly removing my coat and hanging it over the back of my chair. He reaches over and helps me, treating me to another waft of his clean scent.

'Whilst we acknowledge this, we still haven't decided whether or not to reinstate the event,' Mrs. Blackenbury points out from the top of the table. 'There are several factors to consider.'

'Such as?' Klaus's voice is as assertive as hers, and I'm amazed to see how business-like he can be. In fact, one could easily be mistaken for thinking that *he's* the one holding this meeting, and not her.

'Well, there's the costs to begin with,' she says. 'We need to think about the cost of hiring all the stalls, and chairs, the insurance, the time and cost of inviting all the regular stallholders, as well as the manpower for our own stall.'

'*Your* stall?' Klaus narrows his eyes at her.

'Yes, of course. It's a council-run event. We need to have a stall to advertise the local council. Let visitors know who we are and what we do. And reiterate our position to the locals, of course.'

Klaus nods. 'So, all the councillors make themselves known at this stall, do they? A sort of meet and greet affair? Seeing if there's anything the people of the town need to discuss with any of them?'

She balks. 'Well, not exactly. We have leaflets and things with information about the council and all the good we've done this year, and what our plans are for the forthcoming year.'

'And all the councillors attend and hand them out, do they? Making themselves available to discuss any issues the public might have?' Klaus watches her face intently.

'Not exactly,' she replies before swallowing hard.

'As if we'd have time for all that!' One of the men sneers.

'Time for what? The electorate? The people who put you in the position to help the town?' Klaus is on a roll, and several people squirm uncomfortably in their seats.

'We don't just make public appearances,' an elderly lady points out.

'*Just*? It sounds as though you don't do *any*, or am I mistaken?' Klaus frowns.

'Most of our work is done behind the scenes,' another man explains.

'So, do you need a stall at the market or not? Only, it sounds as though it's way too much trouble for you, and if that's the case then wouldn't it be better to give it to someone who will help endorse the Christmas spirit? Someone who might be providing a service or product that fits directly with the whole point of the event? Someone who, no doubt, will be paying for their presence, and so swelling the coffers of the town's funds, enabling you good people to continue your work in helping make improvements to Merryville?'

'Well, when you put it like that, you *do* have a point,' a lady mutters, followed by nods of agreement.

'That solves the problem from the council's point of view, anyway.' Klaus makes it sound like a done deal and I can't help feeling impressed. 'Now, the matter of contacting stall holders can't be a difficult one. You must have a list of previous vendors, who can just be rung up and invited along, surely?'

'Well... I suppose.' Mrs. Blackenbury doesn't seem quite so sure of herself now, and the other councillors just nod.

'So, the other obstacle is the cost.' Klaus glances down at the notepad in front of him, which, incidentally, is blank. 'This is an annual event for which the council has a regular budget, is it not? Surely the market pays for itself, year on year, so the cost of this year's event will be offset by the profits of last year?'

The man sitting to the right of Mrs. Blackenbury nods. 'Of course.'

'So, are there any other problems with holding the German Christmas Market this year?' Klaus clarifies, looking around the table.

No one speaks, but plenty of people shake their heads.

'In that case, can we assume it is going ahead as usual?' Klaus stares directly at Mrs. Blackenbury, as do the rest of the councillors.

She blushes. 'Yes.'

'Good. I'm sure that'll raise morale around here, almost as much as you putting up the lights and decorating the town.' Klaus offers her a smile.

'Well, let's hope so. I just hope it's all worth it.' She doesn't look convinced.

'It will be. Thank you, everyone, for your time,' Klaus says, standing up.

I quickly follow suit, pulling on my coat as several of the attendees come over and shake Klaus's hand. He takes it all in his stride, seemingly oblivious to their impressed expressions. I, however, feel a swell of pride inside me, having just watched a master at work. It certainly offers me even more hope for the rest of my mission—or, rather, *our* mission.

The winter sun bounces off the snow when we go back outside, and it feels slightly warmer than before.

'Well done, in there,' I say to Klaus as we walk away from the Town Hall. 'How did you convince them to put up the town's decorations?'

'I have my ways.' He offers me another of his secretive smiles and my stomach goes all jittery.

'I didn't expect her to call a whole meeting,' I admit.

'I think she just wanted reinforcements once I told her what I needed to discuss.'

I nod. 'Well, I can see you're a whizz with little old ladies, but how are you with big corporations?'

He gives me another smile. 'What do *you* think?'

'I THINK I MIGHT BE FALLING JUST A LITTLE BIT IN LOVE WITH THIS GUY!'

We hop on the next bus heading out of town, feeling quite fired up and ready for action.

'We're going to have to box clever with Jupiter Jumpers,' I tell Klaus in a low voice. 'There's a chance Drew Chapman might recognise me and I certainly don't want to make any trouble for my dad.'

'Leave him to me.' Klaus puts a warm arm around me. 'And, don't forget, we can't say too much or it'll ruin our chances if it goes to court.'

'I just want to confront them and tell them they can't do this to people,' I admit. 'It's just not right and we can't let them get away with it.'

He smiles, rubbing his thumb gently over my shoulder. 'I know. But we can't go in there all guns blazing or it will spoil everything.'

I frown at him. 'What do *you* think we should do, then?'

'We need to get evidence of what they're up to,' he says, decisively. 'Once we can prove what they're doing, we can fight it—or, rather, my dad can.'

I raise my eyebrows. 'Your dad? Do you really think he's interested in helping us? I mean, I know he was asking lots of questions yesterday, but I wasn't sure if he was just being polite. Would he really want to help us save Christmas?'

'I'm sure he'll help us save the factory if he can,' Klaus assures me with a chuckle. 'I'm not so sure about Christmas.'

'It's the same thing,' I reply, matter-of-factly.'

He narrows his eyes, giving me a slightly bemused look. 'Really?'

I nod. 'Oh, yes. It's all part of my plan.' I lower my voice, getting a little closer so he can hear. 'If we can get everyone's jobs back at the factory, they'll all be much happier and want to celebrate. It'll also show everyone else that they've got nothing to fear about all the other companies being taken over by the fat cats over at the trading estate.'

'You think that's what's worrying them?' Klaus looks thoughtful.

I nod. 'Mum told me. They didn't just cancel Christmas because of the jumper factory; it got people worried that if it could happen to Jumpers for Joy then it could happen to all the other companies around here. They're all scared they'll lose their jobs. We'll need to prove that Merryville isn't a place to be messed with.'

'That makes sense.' Klaus nods.

I gape at him. I don't think anyone's ever said that to me before.

'So, you think if we can expose Jupiter Jumpers it'll give the right message to everyone else who might be thinking of using underhand tactics to squeeze the life out of Merryville?' He smiles. 'I hadn't really thought of it that way, but you're absolutely right. We'll set a precedent for the rest of the town.'

Absolutely right? Me? I think I might be falling just a little bit in love with this guy!

'Exactly.' I nod, secretly marvelling at how well Klaus understands me. I'm not used to this at all.

He squeezes my shoulder and we gaze out the window at the Shropshire countryside. It really is the most beautiful county, with swathes of white fields giving way to the majestic mountains of Wales in the distance. There are some large towns here, of course, but the built-up areas are far outweighed by the beautiful, sprawling, rural aspect.

As we near the town of Showford the countryside view gives way to more buildings and busier roads. The bus eats up the miles of grey office blocks and factories until we pull into the side of a busy street opposite the large entrance to Waverley Fields Trading Estate.

My heart's pounding as I grab Klaus's warm hand and we stand up with several others to exit the bus. Outside the weather feels colder, which is surprising given the number of tall buildings surrounding us, which would normally offer some shelter from the icy wind. I wonder if the coldness isn't inside me, rather than outside, as I feel myself shiver, both with the low temperature and the trepidation of what we're about to do.

'I'll do all the talking, if you like?' Klaus offers, pulling me a little closer to him as we cross the street and enter the large estate.

Although I usually love to be the one talking, on this occasion I concede that it might be the best option.

'If you see that Drew-guy you might have to make yourself scarce,' Klaus goes on. 'We don't want to give the game away.'

'True.' I nod as we come to a large sign with a map of the area.

'Okay, Jupiter Jumpers should be just down there.' Klaus points to my right. 'Looks like one of the biggest factories around here.'

It doesn't surprise me. Jumpers for Joy could easily fill one of these massive buildings, but there's no way they'd want to be situated on a trading estate on the outskirts of such a large town. Part of its charm is the countryside setting, and tourists love coming to take a look around. I can't see anyone taking a journey out here just to look around one of these monstrosities. I'll bet the atmosphere inside isn't half as friendly, either. Drew Chapman's welcome to it.

We arrive at the factory and I gape at the sight. It has a domed roof and the large sign outside boasts 'Jupiter Jumpers for Fashion that's Out of this World.' Klaus rolls his eyes and squeezes my hand a little tighter as we venture up the stone steps.

The foyer is vast, and we have to walk quite a way across it to reach the reception desk, where a pretty redhead is smiling at us.

'Good morning. How can I help you?' Her eyes instantly fix on Klaus and she beams.

'Good morning. I'm hoping to speak with the sales director if he's available,' Klaus replies, smiling back at her. 'I'm new to the area and am hoping you'll be able to supply our business.'

Her eyes light up and she nods. 'Of course. If you'd like to take a seat, Mr... er... ?'

'Schmidt,' he offers.

I have to admire his improvisation. There's just a chance that the name Saint might cause suspicions if Drew Chapman were to hear of him. And Smith would be way too obvious.

'Of course, Mr. Schmidt. I'll call him right away.'

'What is his name?' Klaus asks as she lifts the phone receiver.

'Drew Chapman is our sales director, and the sales manager is Terry Greene,' she says, still smiling. 'I'll see which one is available.'

'Terry Greene? I've heard of him.' Klaus says, immediately. 'Do you know where he worked before he came here?'

She nods. 'Yes, he's quite new to us. He was at Mayfield Mills before he came here.'

Klaus wags his finger, frowning. 'That might be where I've met him.'

'If you prefer, I can see if *he's* free?' she offers.

'That would be wonderful.' He gives her another bright smile before leading me towards some large, firm sofas which line one wall.

My heart's hammering as we watch her make the call. Surreptitiously, I scan the area, identifying the ladies' loo in case I need to make a quick escape. Yet again, Klaus's warm hand covers mine; silently assuring me we can handle this.

A man I don't recognize comes out of a lift a few minutes later, smiling as he nears us. 'Mr. Schmidt?'

We both stand and Klaus reaches out a hand to the stranger. 'Good morning.'

'I'm Terry Greene, the sales manager. I hear you're interested in becoming a customer of ours?' He throws us both a warm smile, while shaking hands with Klaus.

'Yes. Thank you so much for seeing me without an appointment, Mr. Greene.'

The man chuckles. 'Terry, please. And it's no problem at all.' His suit looks quite crumpled, and his black hair is quite wayward, though I'm not sure if that's the style or not. He also needs a good shave.

'Klaus,' he replies with a nod. 'This is my assistant, Mary.'

The man manages a smile for me and a nod of the head, but I can see he has no interest in me at all. *Good.*

'It's nice to meet you,' I offer.

'You too, Mary.'

I'll be having a word with Klaus later about my name, too, though I can see from his smirk that he's just done this to wind me up. Game on!

'We have a showroom with most of our designs on display,' Terry goes on, immediately turning his attention back to Klaus.

'I'd love to see it,' Klaus says, nodding as we follow the guy over to the lift.

'Do you have any idea what kind of thing you're looking for?' Terry goes on.

'We're looking for something stylish and classy,' Klaus replies. 'The very best quality, of course.'

'Of course,' Terry repeats. 'I'm sure you'll be impressed by our attention to detail and our quality inspectors are very particular.'

'That's nice to hear.' Klaus nods just as the lift jerks to a halt and the doors slide open.

In front of us are large, glass doors, which Terry opens and we're in a massive room with items of clothing displayed tastefully on the walls, on mannequins and laid out neatly on tables. It resembles a high-end boutique and smells of fresh vanilla.

'We don't just manufacture jumpers,' Terry points out, leading Klaus into the room.

I hang back a little, taking it all in. To the untrained eye it all looks very impressive, and I'm sure plenty of buyers would be thrilled to order large stocks of these items. I peer closely at them, and have to admit the quality of these samples is immaculate.

'Whoa, these are certainly eye-catching,' I hear Klaus say, and look over to see that they've arrived at a large display of Jumpers for Joy.

I catch up with them, though I don't get close enough for Terry to notice me. I'd rather keep under his radar.

'They're rather stunning, aren't they?' Terry smiles. 'This is a new range for us and I have to say, it's been proving very popular. The Christmas designs in particular.'

'So, is this a franchise? I notice the name is different from the rest of your range.' Klaus sounds quite casual as he goes over and touches one of the jumpers, examining the stitching.

'Something like that.' Terry continues to smile, and nods at the item Klaus is inspecting. 'Great, aren't they?'

Klaus nods. 'The quality is very impressive,' he says. 'But it's not made here, then? You sell on behalf of other companies?'

Terry's face reddens in panic and he takes a deep breath. 'No, no, we make everything ourselves, of course. We own this company and as this range is so popular with the businesses they used to supply, we've kept their name on the jumpers, that's all.'

'I see. So you own Jumpers for Joy and make their designs yourselves? I understand.' Klaus smiles.

Terry can't hide his relief as he gives out a big sigh. He smiles back with a nod. 'That's right.'

I follow from a safe distance, checking out their other ranges. Jumpers for Joy seems to be the only range that has labels other than Jupiter Jumpers, and I wonder if it's because the other companies they've stolen designs from were much smaller and didn't have the kudos attached to their brand that Jumpers for Joy has. I can only assume they're planning on buying the name from the Hudsons when they can reach them— or maybe they think it won't matter if the company's already dissolved.

Klaus is a brilliant actor, and seems to know exactly which questions to ask to glean the answers we need.

'Everything is made on the premises?' he asks

Terry, taking an interest in a shawl-necked jumper that looks like cashmere.

'Yes.' Terry isn't quite as convincing as he'd like to think, and I notice he has a tick on his neck that seems to be working overtime. 'We do everything here. The manufacturing takes place in that building at the back of us, and this is where all the management and admin staff are. Of course, some of the sales reps are mobile, but this is your one-stop-shop for everything, so to speak. He gives a little chuckle, while Klaus just nods.

'You distribute from here as well?' Klaus asks, looking impressed. 'I'm surprised you have room for everything here.'

'We own the largest plot on the estate,' Terry boasts. 'Our distribution centre is housed behind the factory, where they have a separate exit from the premises out onto the main road. I could show you around if you like?'

'That would be good, but I don't have time today,' Klaus tells him, much to my relief.

Although it would be very interesting to have a good snoop around the place, the chances of bumping into Drew Chapman would be way too high for my liking. Even in here, I keep wondering if he'll come in to meet this new buyer.

Terry suddenly jumps to action. 'Of course, Klaus, I should have thought. A man like you must be very busy. These companies don't run themselves, do they? Who was it you said you were with again?'

'We are called Schmidt and Son and we've just moved to Shropshire,' Klaus tells him, with a grin. 'And that's not easy to say.' They both chuckle. 'We will be moving to our new premises after Christmas, which is why I was eager to get my stock ordered as soon as possible.'

'Of course,' Terry gushes. 'Let's go to my office so we can fill out the paperwork.'

We follow him out of the showroom and down the corridor to a small office with a slightly musty smell. It looks quite bare and I get the impression it isn't used as much as one might expect. I wonder if Terry Greene usually conducts his business from his car as he touts companies for business.

'Do sit down,' he offers, unlocking a drawer of his dusty desk.

We sit opposite him and he pulls out a pile of forms. My heart sinks. Klaus is going to have to do a good job of convincing him that we're for real with that lot to complete. For the first time, I see the blonde Adonis next to me swallow hard, and a flash of panic runs through my veins. Klaus is out of his comfort zone.

'Now, I just need to take down some details about your company,' Terry says, suddenly sounding quite officious. He opens up the first form, which is full of tiny writing that can hardly be read with the naked eye —and that's not even the small print!

Glancing around the room I notice several papers lying on the cabinets to the side of me, and crane my neck to see what they are when I think Terry's too ensconced in the form to notice. Some kind of delivery notes are in one pile, with more very official-looking forms next to them.

'Credit references?' I hear Klaus saying. 'Of course. I'll get them sent over to you.'

He's struggling!

'Ooh!' I put a hand to my head.

'Are you all right?' Klaus immediately turns to me, putting a warm hand on my arm.

I sit back in my seat, praying I look convincing.

'Do you have any water?' Klaus asks Terry, with a concerned edge to his voice.

'I'll get some.' Terry quickly jumps up and leaves the room.

I point to the papers on the cabinet and we both rush over and take photos of everything we can find. One of the forms is quite lengthy so I grab it and a delivery note and thrust them into my bag before returning to my seat as I hear footsteps hurrying up the corridor.

'Here.' Terry offers the glass to Klaus, who puts a hand on my cheek before helping me take a sip of the cold water.

'She's burning up,' Klaus tells Terry. 'She's only just got over the flu. I think maybe she's come back to work a little too early.'

'Oh, right.' Terry suddenly looks quite alarmed, and I'm not convinced it's my health that's got him so rattled.

Klaus puts the glass on the table. 'I'm going to have to take her home,' he announces firmly.

'Oh, but the order...?' Terry splutters.

'I'll take the forms with me and get them back to you this afternoon,' Klaus says. 'But I really don't want Mary to start vomiting like she did last time. It wasn't pleasant, I can assure you.'

Terry's eyes almost pop out of his head as he leaps to his feet, offering Klaus the forms. 'Of course. Call me; my number's in there.' He thrusts the papers into Klaus's hand, before my guy quickly leads me towards the door.

Just as we reach it, it flings open. My heart sinks.

'Hello. I'm Drew Chapman.'

7

———

**'IT'S NOT MY FAULT GUCCI DON'T
OFFER A VOMIT-RESISTANT FINISH'**

That old saying about being careful what you wish for springs to my mind—while something really horrid rises in my throat. I was only pretending to feel ill to get us out of a tight spot, but now it's just become a dreadful reality. I must have been so worried about bumping into Drew that it's all become too much.

I'm keeping my head down to avoid being recognised, but it seems to be escalating the churning of my stomach, and now the back of my throat's burning.

'It's good to meet you, Mr. Chapman,' Klaus says quickly, 'But I'm afraid my—'

Too late! My lovely breakfast has just reappeared all over Drew Chapman's suede loafers.

'Aah!' He leaps backwards and I can only imagine

his horror as I immediately perform a mighty impressive encore.

This time it hits the floor, splashing up his trousers. The poor guy gives another yelp, and Terry rushes towards us, spouting platitudes to his boss, while Klaus offers me a tissue to wipe my mouth.

'We need to go. Sorry about the... erm...' Klaus ushers me past the mess and I notice Mr. Chapman gives me a wide berth as we hurry towards the lift.

Once on our own, away from that situation, I start to feel much better. Klaus has his arm around me—which I feel is really brave of him, given the circumstances—and is reassuring me everything will be all right. I quickly check my clothes to make sure I didn't vomit on any of them, and am relieved that I seem to have escaped the fallout, so to speak.

'Are you okay?' Klaus asks me gently as we reach the ground floor.

I nod. 'I don't think I'm going to be sick again.'

'Yeah, I'd be surprised if you've got anything left in your system after all that,' he agrees.

I'm not really sure how to take his remark, but thinking back to the state of the floor of that corridor —and Drew Chapman's expensive-looking shoes—I think he might be right.

'We'll get a taxi home,' Klaus goes on, as we exit the building and the cold air greets us.

I take long, deep breaths, which immediately helps me feel less nauseous.

'A taxi? That'll cost a small fortune,' I reply, frowning.

'It'll be much more comfortable for you, and we'll be able to stop if you need to.' He sounds like he's already made his mind up. 'And I'm paying, so don't worry about it. It's the least I can do.'

I smile at him. 'That's really kind of you.'

He holds me a little tighter and, again, I admire his courage.

'Not really.' He chuckles, pulling out his phone once we're a safe distance from the factory. 'Honestly, I haven't had this much fun in ages. You should have seen Drew Chapman's face when you barfed all over his Gucci's. I don't think he'll forget us in a hurry—much as he'll want to, no doubt.'

Gucci's? I *knew* they were expensive!

'Well I'm glad it gave you something to laugh about,' I snap.

His eyes widen as he looks down at me. 'Hey, I'm sorry. I didn't mean it like that.' Then a smile teases his lips. 'But, honestly, Chris, it *was* funny.'

'I was terrified he'd recognise me,' I point out. 'Honestly, if he saw my face—'

'I'm sure it wasn't your face he was worried about,' Klaus assures me, evidently trying not to giggle.

I roll my eyes. It was clearly entertaining from his

point of view, but I've never felt so embarrassed in my life. Throwing up all over Drew Chapman was bad enough, but did it *have* to be right in front of Klaus? I'm relieved he doesn't seem grossed out by the whole thing—unlike Drew Chapman, of course—but I really wish I'd controlled myself, at least until we'd left the building and I could have made a run for it before he had to witness me puking my guts up.

Klaus rings for a taxi, arranging to meet it further down the road, and then returns his phone to his pocket with a grin. 'Well, my phone certainly came in handy in that place,' he says. 'I managed to record the whole conversation in the showroom. That'll come in really handy, I'm sure.'

I gape at him. 'You recorded it all? I hadn't even thought of that.'

'I'm a very thoughtful person.' He smiles modestly.

Although I smile in agreement, I decide not to say anything. I think that gorgeous head of his would burst if I stroked his ego any more. And, besides, I still haven't forgotten him introducing me as Mary.

I'm glad to get as far from the factory as I can, as we make our way down the busy street.

'You did really well in there,' he says, as we sit down on a bench set apart from the road a short way. 'Honestly, noticing those papers on the cabinet was a stroke of genius.'

I gape at him. 'I wonder if they've noticed we took

some of them. Maybe we should get a bit farther away from the place in case they come after us.'

He smiles, shaking his head. 'Why would they? There were enough papers there; they probably won't notice any are missing for quite a while yet. And I gave them a completely fictitious address, so they can hardly look us up, can they?'

I sigh, hoping he's right.

'The taxi will be here any minute, anyway,' Klaus assures me. 'We'll be well away before anyone suspects anything—if they ever do. And don't forget, they've got other things to worry about right now. Like how to get vomit out of Gucci suede.' He chuckles, holding me a little closer.

'You're not going to let me forget this, are you?' I narrow my eyes at him and can't help noticing how relaxed and handsome he looks.

'Nope.'

'That's what I thought.'

I delve into my bag and pull out a bottle of perfume which I quickly spray over myself, hoping to get rid of any lingering 'eau de barf' before we get into the taxi. I'm pretty sure I wouldn't be allowed in if the driver knew what had just happened.

Luckily, we get a cheerful driver who chatters to Klaus most of the way, leaving me to doze in the warmth, and giving time for my stomach to settle completely before we reach home.

. . .

THE RICH SMELL of warm gingerbread greets us as soon as we go into the kitchen, and Mum smiles as soon as she sees us.

'With all these decorations I was really in the mood for some festive baking,' she chirps. 'You're just in time to taste the first batch.'

Usually, there's nothing I'd love more than to tuck into Mum's home baking, but my stomach gurgles dangerously and I quickly run out of the room and dive upstairs to the bathroom. Luckily, I'm not actually sick again, but take the opportunity to clean my teeth several times and wash my face.

Even though I can't find a single trace of vomit on my clothes, I can still smell it on me, somehow, so I strip off and change into a different outfit. I also tie my hair in a high ponytail, so it's off my face. It makes me feel better, if nothing else.

As I make my way back downstairs I can hear Mum and Klaus laughing in the kitchen. They're sitting at the large table cradling mugs of something hot, and munching gingerbread.

'How are you feeling, love?' Mum offers me a sympathetic smile when she sees me return. 'Klaus said you've been poorly.'

'Better than I was, thanks.' I eye them both a little

warily, wondering if I was the subject of their earlier hysterics.

'You look nice.' Klaus smiles kindly as I take the seat next to him.

'Thanks. I just needed to freshen up a bit.'

'Are those jeans a good idea?' Mum asks, doubtfully.

Trust her! I've pulled on a pair of white jeans and an oversized jumper with Father Christmas and a robin on the front.

'They'll be fine, Mum. Honestly, I don't think I could be sick again if I tried—not that I'd want to. I think it was probably just nerves that caused it. I'm all right now.'

'Well, I suppose that's more than can be said for Drew Chapman,' Mum replies, thoughtfully.

'It's not *my* fault Gucci don't offer a vomit-resistant finish for their suede loafers,' I grouch, realising what they must have been laughing about earlier. I somehow knew I'd be the butt of their joke.

'I'd love to have been a fly on the wall,' Mum says with a giggle.

'You'd be safer on the ceiling, Mrs. Moss. That stuff went everywhere,' Klaus chuckles. 'Honestly, your daughter could barf for England.'

I roll my eyes. I can't really blame them; if it hadn't been quite so humiliating I might have found it funny myself. I go over to the sink to pour myself a glass of water, still feeling the burn in the back of my throat.

There's a choking sound as I turn on the cold tap, then it splutters into life, sending a gush of water all over me.

'Aah!' My hand slips on the tap as I fumble with it, trying to turn it off, but I must be turning it the wrong way as more water forces itself into my face and soaks my jumper. It's zooming out like a geyser—and right in my direction.

'What *are* you doing?' Mum asks, incredulously.

'Drowning!' I shout back.

My feet slide under me and I realise I'm not the only thing getting wet. I just know I'm about to slide right onto my backside—can this day get any worse?

Just as I'm losing all hope I feel a strong arm holding me up, while Klaus's hand comes over mine on the tap and he easily turns it off.

'Are you all right?' To give him his due, he looks genuinely concerned, despite the little smile teasing the corners of his mouth.

'I'm drenched,' I tell him, nodding.

'Look at the state of you!' Mum raises her eyebrows.

'It was the tap,' I protest.

'It was fine earlier,' she informs me. 'What did you do to it?'

'*Me*?' I gawp at her.

'Maybe you should go and get changed before you

catch your death,' Klaus suggests, calmly. 'I'll clean up here.'

'Thanks,' I reply, nodding as I drip past him and head for the door.

'I did wonder about those jeans.' Mum shakes her head as I squelch past her.

Not only is my throat sore, but now my tongue is, too—I've had to bite it so hard!

'ARE YOU SURE YOU'RE OKAY?' Klaus asks when I return to the table a short while later.

I've had another complete change of clothes, this time into a pair of black jeans, and a green and white jumper with Christmas trees all over it. It might sound boring, but it's actually really pretty. *I* like it, anyway.

I manage a smile. 'Yeah. Thanks ever so much for your help.'

He grins, rubbing his hand over mine. 'Anytime.'

'Are you sure you won't try some gingerbread?' Mum offers. 'Just a little bit can't do any harm, surely?'

I shake my head. 'No thanks, Mum. Honestly, I don't want to chance it just yet.'

She sighs. 'Well, I'm sure all this will put a smile on your dad's face, anyway,' she says. 'He's been a bit down lately, with this factory business.'

'It's understandable,' Klaus offers, sympathetically.

'That reminds me. We picked up some papers while we were at Jupiter's,' I say, jumping up, and going back into the hall where I left my bag with my coat. I come back with a handful of crumpled up forms and put them on the table.'

'What's this?' Mum frowns, picking one up.

'I'm not really sure. They were in Terry Greene's office. He's the sales manager over there.'

Klaus and I both pick up some papers and take a look.

'Looks like a delivery note,' Klaus says. 'You were right.'

I frown, squinting to read the small print at the bottom of the page near the customer's signature. 'Mum, have you got a magnifying glass?'

'Maybe you need to put your specs on,' she tells me, going over to the kitchen drawer.

'I don't even think *they'd* be much help for this,' I reply, holding it up to show her how tiny the writing is.

Mum grimaces. 'That's even smaller than the newsprint your dad uses this for.'

I take it from her and test it out to find the right distance to read it. My jaw just about hits the floor when I realise what it says. 'This is to confirm that the signee of the above company agrees to be supplied by Jupiter Jumpers as from 10th December 2021,' I read aloud.

'Oh no.' Mum puts a hand to her mouth.

'I'll bet the person who signed it didn't read it,' Klaus says, taking it from me. 'To all intents and purposes it just looks like a regular delivery note.'

Heat rises in my face. 'Look who it's from,' I say, pointing. 'Poulson's Pullovers. There's no way Frank would have signed it knowingly.'

'It's probably not his signature,' Klaus points out. 'But what does this say?'

I put the magnifying glass over the part he indicates, which is a tiny line of writing under the signature.

'Signed by, or on behalf of, the managing director.' I gape. 'They wouldn't have realised that when they signed it, I'm sure of it.'

Klaus flips the page over. 'Look, it was someone called Bill Wystanstowe.' Sure enough, there was another box asking for the printed name of the signee.

'I've never heard of him,' I say with a shrug.

'Well, he's hardly likely to be one of the managers,' Mum interjects. 'Isn't it usually someone from the warehouse who would sign for deliveries? Especially large ones.'

I nod. 'That's true. There's no way anyone who had the authority to change suppliers would be the person to take in deliveries. They're totally different jobs.' My stomach feels all jittery and I take deep breaths in case it's anything more sinister than a few nerves.

'I'll get my dad to look into this,' Klaus says. 'He'll be able to tell if it's legal or not.'

'I think we should go and speak to Frank Poulson,' I say, standing up. 'It'll be interesting to see what he's got to say about all this. I wonder if he's even got a copy.'

'We'll take this one with us. I'll photograph it for my dad,' Klaus says, 'we've got the other stuff to send over to him anyway. You know, the pictures we took while we were there.'

Mum puts her hand to her mouth. 'Oh no. You didn't take pictures of all that...?' She pales at the thought—and with good reason.

'Ew! You mean the... *mess*?' I cringe. 'No, Mum. We didn't take any photos of that!'

8

'I CAN'T BELIEVE I LET JUPITER JUMPERS PULL THE WOOL OVER MY EYES'

The snow's falling again as our taxi pulls in at Merryville station and it's turned even colder.

'Oh no, it's another half an hour before the next train to Craven Head,' I moan, checking out the timetable.

We buy our tickets at the machine, disappointed that it's even too crowded for us to sit down anywhere on the station platform.

'I was telling your mum about the town council meeting,' Klaus says with a grin, as he takes my hand. 'Why don't we go and spread the word while we've got some time to kill?'

'I'd almost forgotten about that,' I admit, following him out of the station.

'Let's just pop into here first,' he says, as we pass a small boutique.

I raise my eyebrows, but don't like to say anything, as I follow him inside. It's much warmer in the shop and I'm tempted to take a look at the clothes, but can't tear my eyes from Klaus as he strides confidently up to the counter.

'Good afternoon. Are you the manager?' he asks the lady at the till.

'Yes, can I help you?' She smiles at him. *I've noticed women do that a lot, actually.*

'I just thought you'd want to know that Christmas is back on in Merryville. I was in a meeting at the Town Hall earlier where they're making preparations for the German Christmas Market, and they're also going to decorate the town.

'Merryville Toys is having a large festive display in the window, and I just thought you might like to follow suit.' He sounds utterly charming as he tells her, and I can see she's totally captivated by him, as well as his words.

'Really?' Her eyes widen.

He nods. 'Perhaps you could help spread the word?'

She beams at him. 'Of course. And I'll get our decorations out this afternoon. To be honest, it's much better for business. In fact, I think I've got some

Christmas music I can put on in the meantime. A nice bit of Bublé. It helps get the staff in the mood, too.'

By 'the staff' I think she means 'her', judging by the dreamy expression on her face.

'Great. Thank you.' He grins and leads me back out of the shop.

'Once Mrs. Blackenbury's got all the advertising leaflets organised for the German Market, we'll have to help distribute them,' he says. 'I think the shops are a good place to start, don't you?'

'I wonder if anyone's contacted the local radio station yet. Or the press.' I've suddenly gone back into work mode as I consider getting the word out.

'Good thinking. We could call them on the journey over to Craven Head.' He nods, and I think I've impressed him.

We manage to fit in a few more shops before I notice the time, and we have to run back to the station. Luckily, Klaus holds on to me to save me falling in the slippery snow as we rush to the platform, which isn't half as crowded as when we left. The train's already waiting for us, and we hop on quickly, just before the whistle is blown. It's not very busy, and we manage to find a couple of seats with a table.

We call the media while we're whizzing through the countryside, and inform the reporters about the change of plan for Merryville. We spend some time convincing them that Christmas is most certainly back on in the town, and that we're looking forward to welcoming anyone who'd like to visit.

'I hope we're not too late to drum up some interest,' I say, a little gloomily, once we're finished. 'I mean, people who have heard that Christmas is cancelled may well have made other plans by now. What if we do all this and no one comes?'

'They'll come.' Klaus places a warm, reassuring hand on mine, and smiles.

There's something quite mysterious and knowing about his expression, and I can't fail to believe him.

We sit, hand in hand for a while, looking out at the snow-covered open fields ,and the white mountains seem even closer from here. There's no noise except the whirr of the train as it speeds along, and we sit in a comfortable silence with our thoughts. Being so close to Klaus helps my confidence, somehow, and I really feel like we're completely on the same page.

'Here we are,' he says, as we pull up at Craven Head Station. It's decorated just as I'd hoped Merryville's would be, with bright lights and sparkling tinsel everywhere. Their tree isn't as big as one would have expected, and it seems to be weighed down with all the decorations piled onto it. Everything looks bright and cheery and, along with the music blaring from the speakers in between rail announcements, the place has a very exciting, festive vibe.

I've never been to Poulson's Pullovers before, and

check out the directions on my phone as we head up the crowded street. A brass band is belting out Christmas hymns in the large, open square, which is full of people watching and singing along.

'This is how it should be at Merryville,' I comment, shouting above the volume.

'It will be.' Klaus always seems so sure of himself, and I just hope he's right.

I notice the large building on the corner and point. 'There it is.' It would have been hard to miss it, in all honesty, as Poulson's Pullovers is huge. We quicken our pace as we near it. It's teaming with customers and there are long queues at the tills. Although it's warmer inside, it's not too warm that I feel the need to peel off my coat. I assume it's a canny way to encourage shoppers to buy the jumpers while also saving on the heating bills. *Clever!*

Christmas songs ring out, and customers can be seen singing along, and some are even having a little dance as they peruse the multitude of pullovers on sale. The whole shop is a riot of colour and a hive of activity. Everyone seems to be smiling, and it's obvious business is doing well.

Klaus and I take some time to examine some of the stock, and I recognise a few of the designs from Jumpers for Joy. I have mixed feelings as I study them. I'm glad that Frank Poulson is doing so well, of course, but can't help feeling a little hurt that Dad and all the others at the factory have had to lose their jobs, albeit allegedly.

'There's Frank.' I notice the tall, grey-haired man who used to spend lots of time at our house while I was growing up. He was a really close friend of Dad, and I hate to think that's all changed now. He's dressed in a very smart suit with a V-neck Christmas sweater under his jacket. He must have heard his name, as he turns and his face lights up when he sees me.

'Chrissy, how are you?' He gushes as he comes over to us, his arms outspread.

'Hi Frank. I'm fine, thanks. This is my friend Klaus,' I tell him after a brief hug.

Klaus reaches out a hand to shake his, and Frank smiles warmly at him.

'Doing some Christmas shopping?' Frank asks.

'Actually, we wanted to have a word with you, if that's all right?' I suddenly feel a little nervous. Frank seems just as friendly as he's always been, which doesn't add up, somehow.

'Of course.' He nods, then frowns. 'Everything is okay with your parents, I hope?'

'Physically, yes,' I reply.

He narrows his eyes. 'Shall we go and get some hot chocolate?'

'That would be lovely.'

We follow him up the escalator to where a large café stands on a mezzanine level, overlooking the sales floor. Heavenly smells of chocolate, coffee, and cinnamon greet us as we reach the top and Frank nods at a waitress who leads us over to a vacant table.

The range of delights is phenomenal, and I choose a hot chocolate with marshmallows, cream and sprinkles, while Klaus opts for a spicy one.

'And warm mince pies with plenty of clotted cream, please, Julie,' Frank says, with a smile.

'Of course, sir.'

'I must say, I've been very remiss in not contacting your Dad for quite a while,' Frank begins, looking quite rueful. 'It's just been so busy around here, but that's no excuse not to look in on an old friend. Do give him my regards when you see him, and tell him I'll definitely be in touch very soon. Perhaps he and your mum would like to come out for a drink with us over Christmas? I know Fiona would also love to catch up with them.'

'I'm sure they'd appreciate that, Frank.' I nod, looking up as Julie returns with a tray full of goodies.

Frank passes around our drinks and puts the tray of mince pies in the centre of the table for us to help ourselves. Some are iced—my favourite—while others are just dusted in icing sugar. There's a huge bowl of clotted cream, and I'm quite flattered that Frank must have remembered my penchant for Cornwall's finest.

Klaus and I moan our appreciation of the gorgeous pies and drinks, and Frank smiles.

'You know you're welcome to come here for free mince pies and hot chocolate anytime,' he assures me. 'But something tells me that's not all you're here for.' He narrows his eyes again.

'You're right.' I put the very small remainder of my mince pie on the plate in front of me and wipe my mouth with a napkin. 'It's about the jumpers from Dad's factory.'

He raises his eyebrows. 'Really?'

I nod. 'Frank, did you knowingly return your order to Jumpers for Joy and take delivery of the stock from Jupiter Jumpers instead? You've signed over to using Jupiter's instead of Dad's firm for all future orders. Dad's factory's had to close, not just because you did that, but because other companies followed suit. They lost everything.' I sniff hard as I feel my face flush and tears threaten the corners of my eyes. Klaus immediately places his warm hand on top of mine.

Frank stares at me. '*What*?'

He looks incredulous and something makes my insides go all jittery. They're doing that a lot today, and it's more than a little unnerving.

'You know I'd never do a thing like that,' he goes on, looking slightly hurt at the suggestion. 'Jupiter Jumpers took over Jumpers for Joy, didn't they? I wanted to continue giving my business to your dad's firm, of course, so I just accepted it.'

I shake my head, really fighting the urge to burst

into tears now. 'No. Jupiter Jumpers is a big firm outside of town, who have stolen all the business from Dad's place. That's why they had to shut down Jumpers for Joy. Now all the other companies in Merryville are scared that they'll have to close too, because of the new trading estate, and they cancelled Christmas because of it.' After blurting it all out, I give a loud sniff.

Frank shakes his head. 'That can't be. You must be mistaken.'

'It's true, sir,' Klaus offers, calmly. 'We spent a couple of hours this morning convincing the town council to reinstate the German Christmas Market this year. They'd cancelled all the usual events, and even decided not to put up the Christmas lights.'

Frank looks horrified as he gawps at us. 'That wasn't my understanding at all,' he says. 'I spoke to Drew Chapman personally. He said they'd taken over Jumpers for Joy who would still continue to supply us, just under the new company's name.' He squints in thought for a moment. 'Are you telling me that the order I received *wasn't* from your dad's company?'

I nod. 'Dad said they sent your consignment over but the delivery man got turned away because you'd already received it.'

A look of realisation crosses Frank's face and he closes his eyes momentarily. 'That explains it.'

'What?' A feeling of dread creeps up on me, and Klaus squeezes my hand, as though he can sense it.

Frank lets out a long breath, then sits forward. 'We had a couple of returns,' he tells us in a low voice. 'It's the first time it's ever happened.'

'From Jumpers for Joy?' I stare at him. They've always prided themselves on the high quality of their work, and no one has ever returned one of their products.

He nods slowly. 'Well, the company that claims to be representing them, anyway. They even had the labels in from your dad's firm. And the patterns were exactly what we'd ordered.'

'So Drew Chapman has stolen the patterns and is passing them off as the same,' Klaus states. 'That's illegal.'

'But if their work is substandard and they're passing it off as Jumpers for Joy, what's that going to do for their reputation? How can Dad resurrect the company if they've lost everything they stand for?' I breathe in deeply, unable to hide the sob that catches in my throat.

Klaus rubs his thumb over the back of my hand, soothingly. 'We need to prove what Jupiter Jumpers are up to and take them to court. We sue for damages and defamation, and make darn sure the papers report on it. Not only will it cripple Jupiter Jumpers, but it will clear the name of Jumpers for Joy and give them a shed load of good publicity to boot.'

Frank nods. 'I'll get my sales manager to see what

we've got in writing from that damn company about the so-called takeover. I'll also get my staff to remove all of that order from sale. I don't want my name associated with anything from Jupiter Jumpers, and I never will.'

'Actually, we've managed to get a copy of one of your delivery notes,' Klaus says, as I delve into my bag for the crumpled sheet. 'As you can see, someone here signed on behalf of you to agree to all future orders being fulfilled by Jupiter's.'

'Really?' Frank squints at the signature. 'Who did?'

'The name's printed on the back, sir,' Klaus offers.

Frank turns over the page and gapes at it. 'That's one of the warehouse staff. They can sign for deliveries but they don't have the right to make any management decisions.'

'It's in the small print,' Klaus explains.

'*Miniscule* print, more like.' Frank frowns. 'So this is their game, is it?'

'Do you want me to check if Dad's still got your order at the factory? He could send it over so you won't be short of stock *and* you'll have the quality products you wanted.' The idea comes to me in a flash of inspiration. *And that's something that doesn't happen very often!*

Frank nods, standing up. 'Tell him to send me everything he's got over there. I'll be giving him a call later; I just want to get some answers for him first.'

'Thanks so much, Frank.' This time I give him a big hug, which makes him chuckle.

'Thank *you*,' he replies, smiling. 'I didn't know how to tell your father about the returns, to be honest. And I should have known better than to have believed they came from him in the first place. I owe him a huge apology but first I want to get him some kind of explanation for all this. I hope he's got a good lawyer, because the poor guy's going to be working overtime with all this.'

Klaus beams. 'He's got the best. And he won't mind the extra work one bit.' Klaus stands and shakes Frank's hand again.

'Great. Well I've got a few calls to make. Finish up the pies before you go.' Frank gestures to the table. 'And let Julie know if you want anything else. On the house, of course.'

'Thanks, Frank.' I suddenly feel much better.

'It's the least I can do. I can't believe I let Jupiter Jumpers pull the wool over my eyes.' He shakes his head. 'But they certainly won't get away with it.'

9

'YOU'RE LUCKY YOU'RE NOT IN CASUALTY,'

We both rang our dads in between bites of those delicious mince pies, and now Klaus and I are heading back towards the train station. It's getting dark already and lights are starting to twinkle around the street. I shiver as it's also become much colder.

'We still need to speak to all the shopkeepers and get them to put up their decorations,' I say with a sigh as we fight our way through the crowds. 'And do you think Mrs. Blackenbury will have contacted the stall-holders for the German Market yet?'

'Probably. She'll want to save face now that it's going ahead.' He puts his arm around me and leads me towards a bench on the draughty platform. 'Shall I see if that vending machine's got any hot chocolate?'

I nod. I know it won't be half as good as the ones we

had earlier, but I could do with something to warm me up. We peeped into the station café on our way past, but it's so crowded we'd never get a drink before the train comes.

He returns a few minutes later with a couple of polystyrene cups and hands one to me.

'I can't guarantee it'll be that nice, but at least it's hot,' he says with a self-deprecating smile.

I'm grateful for something warm to wrap my hands around, besides anything else, and grin as he sits next to me.

'It's really good of your dad to help out with the factory business,' I say, shuffling a little closer to him so we're actually touching each other.

He smiles, putting his arm around my shoulder. 'He's happy to have something to get his teeth into,' he replies. 'He felt obliged to close the firm early when Grandma and Grandad announced they were coming to stay with us for a few weeks over Christmas, and I think he's missing having something to do.'

'It must be hard for him, not being able to get excited about the festive season,' I muse.

'That's why they come to us every year,' Klaus says with a smile. 'To force Dad to take an interest whether he likes it or not. Grandma doesn't think it's right for him to wallow in the past, and always worries that I won't have a good time if Dad isn't in the mood for it.' He shrugs. 'They're probably right. With those two around it's impossible not to get caught up in the festivities, though.' He smiles.

'I'm glad. I mean, I know it must be hard with the memories of your mum and all, but I'm sure she wouldn't want you not to celebrate Christmas because of her.' I take a sip of my drink, which tastes quite awful, but I'm still thankful for it.

'That's what Grandma always says. Mum used to love Christmas, so we should honour her memory by making it as joyful as we can, even though she's not here.'

'Your Grandma's a wise woman.'

He chuckles. 'That she is.'

'Dad was really thrilled about Frank.' I can't help remembering how excited he sounded on the phone when I spoke to him.

'I'm just glad we've got to the bottom of it all,' Klaus admits. 'It was obvious something was amiss, but I never suspected that Drew Chapman-guy of doing anything like that.'

'I just hope your dad can sue him and get the good name of the company back before it's too late. You know what they say; mud sticks.' I shake my head.

'Yeah, well with any luck it'll be Jupiter Jumpers that suffers because of all this; not your dad's place.' Klaus helps me up as the train pulls into the station, and stands back to allow me to get on before him.

The warmth greets us as we step inside the carriage

and we snuggle up once we find a vacant seat. It's much busier than it was on the way over here, but I like the excited atmosphere as everyone's chatting and showing each other their shopping.

'I just wish it was a little more like this in Merryville,' I say with a sigh.

Klaus just smiles.

WHEN WE ARRIVE at Merryville Station I stare out the window. Lights have been strewn across the platform, the outside of the café has been decorated with tinsel and more fairy lights, and a large tree has been erected near the entrance.

'Come on, we need to get off,' Klaus cajoles me with a knowing smile.

I gape at his handsome face. 'How did all this happen?'

'It seems Mrs Blackenbury at the council was a little more persuasive than we gave her credit for,' he says, taking my hand and leading me through the crowd to get off the train.

It's early evening, and still the place seems much busier than usual. We have to dodge a few ladders where people are securing the large tree, and beginning to decorate it, but I don't mind one bit. It's lovely to see the station back to normal for this time of year, though I'm still finding it hard to believe it's all happening.

When we get out into the square another surprise awaits me. Not only is there a group of carol singers, which has drawn quite a large crowd, but the Christmas street lights are being positioned, too.

Some of the houses already have wreaths on the doors and we spy decorations and fairy lights inside where people haven't yet drawn their curtains. *Not that I'm nosey or anything, of course.*

'Word certainly travels fast around here,' I comment happily as we pass yet another shop with a lovely Christmassy display in the lit-up window. 'Do you think the lady at the boutique spoke to all these people already?'

Klaus smiles. 'She'd only need to tell one person who passes the word on to another, and the chain goes on,' he says. Then he leans a little closer and tells me in a quiet voice 'though I have heard that the woman in the clothes shop is a bit of a gossip.'

'I take it your shop's decorated?' I ask Klaus, as the thought suddenly occurs to me. I've never known the toy shop not to look spectacular at this time of year, but then, this Christmas is turning out to be unlike any other.

'Of course.' He looks at me as though I'm mad. I get that a lot, for some reason.

Although I'm tempted to reply, I get the distinct

impression it might be best not to. I keep my mouth shut.

The snow starts falling again and I shiver with the cold.

'Come on, let's grab a taxi and get you home,' Klaus insists, casually linking his arm through mine.

When we arrive back at my place, I'm delighted to see that Nick's come over and is talking with Dad at the kitchen table. They've got all sorts of important-looking documents spread out in front of them, and Nick seems to be making lots of notes.

'You're back.' Dad beams at me as we join them, and Mum looks over from the side counter where she's pouring out cups of tea.

'Yeah. And guess what? They're decorating the town and putting up lights.' I smile at them.

'You managed to speak to that woman at the Town Hall, then?' Nick looks up at Klaus.

'Yeah. I think I managed to persuade her.' Klaus grins.

'Evidently,' his dad replies, nodding.

'Sit down. I was just making another cuppa,' Mum says, happily.

Klaus and I remove our coats and boots and sit down. It's always warm and welcoming in our kitchen; I think it's my favourite place to be in the whole world —apart from in Klaus's arms, of course.

'What's all this?' I eye the papers in front of us.

'Proof that the contracts all belong with Jumpers for Joy, and not Drew Chapman,' Dad says. 'He had no right to take them.'

'Frank thought he was still dealing with you,' I reply.

Dad nods. 'I know. He rang me just a short while ago. Explained the whole thing.' He shakes his head. 'It's just one massive debacle, if you ask me.'

'He said the jumpers they got from Jupiter aren't as good quality as our ones.' *I know it's Dad's job, but I still feel an affinity to the place.*

'But they've still got your labels inside,' Klaus points out.

Nick nods with a small smile. 'So we heard. Which is just one of the many crimes we're going to get them with. We've got quite a list so far.'

'But will we be able to do anything about it in time?' I ask, before biting my lip. 'I mean, they've already closed down the factory and everyone's lost their jobs. Will we be able to get them back in time for Christmas?'

Mum joins us and Dad scoots some papers out of the way so she can put the tea tray down. She immediately starts pouring the drinks and passing them round. Nick swiftly gathers up more of the papers before we put our cups on the table.

'We've already got the place open,' Dad says with a smile. 'Frank wants all the stock we can give him, so we've got people over there now packing it all up and loading the vans. And guess what? Frank spread the word to all our other firms who've all said the same thing. They want us to send over their orders right away, and are removing all the Jupiter stock from their shelves. We've had to get the production team working again already to meet the demand.'

'Oh Dad, that's wonderful!' I jump up to go to give him a big hug, but manage to knock my cup which tips over and I only just leap back in time to avoid hot tea spilling all over me.

Mum rolls her eyes, gets up and fetches a cloth to wipe up the mess. I just gape at it, trying to figure out what just happened.

'Well, don't just stand there,' Mum says. 'Grab the mop.'

'I think I'm in shock,' I mumble, but do as she says.

'You're lucky you're not in Casualty,' Dad points out, shaking his head. 'That stuff's hot. You could have scalded yourself.'

'Here, let me help.' Klaus takes the mop from me and quickly cleans the floor while Mum finishes wiping the table and pours me another cup.

'Good job you moved all those papers,' I tell Dad.

'It was no coincidence, love,' he assures me.

I narrow my eyes at him, but say nothing. It's often safer that way.

We're soon all sitting back down drinking tea and

eating the fruit cake that Mum calls her 'tester' for the actual Christmas cake. It's a little smaller than the one we'll have on the big day, and although it has marzipan and icing on, it isn't as elaborately decorated as the 'real' one. It's every bit as delicious, though, and always gets us into the festive spirit. Whether that's down to the cake, or all the booze it contains, is another matter.

'The HR manager's been on the phone letting everyone know their jobs are still intact, and asking them to come into work as soon as they can to help out,' Mum informs me and Klaus.

'I'll bet they're relieved,' Klaus offers.

'Everyone is,' she says with a nod.

'Dave Hesketh, the head of logistics, certainly has his work cut out for him,' Dad adds with a grin. 'And Keith Polter, the distributions manager hasn't stopped rushing around since he got there.'

'I'll bet. What about the accounts department?' I ask, imagining the nightmare of re-issuing all the invoices.

'As long as everyone pulls together, I reckon you can make it work,' Nick says, smiling confidently at Dad. 'You've got a good, strong team there, by the sounds of it.'

Dad nods. 'They're a good bunch. It was awful thinking we'd all lost everything like that, but it's amazing how they've all rallied around today to make this happen.'

'Jupiter Jumpers will get a visit from the Trading Standards Department first thing in the morning,' Nick says, with a grin. 'I reckon they'll shut the place down, at least while they make their enquiries.' He turns to his son. 'You did well recording that conversation today. Getting Terry Greene to admit what they were up to was a master-stroke, and with the physical evidence of those invoices as well, I'd be surprised if we haven't got them banged to rights.'

I stare at him. 'You've managed to act on all of that already?'

'There was no time to waste,' Nick informs me, with an incredulous expression. 'The sooner we got the ball rolling, the sooner we could get Jumpers for Joy back in action.'

'Well, we've certainly done that,' Mum pipes up with a smile. 'In fact, we're all going down there after dinner to lend a hand.'

It wasn't exactly what I had in mind for this evening, but I can see that it makes sense. After all, it was my idea to get all this going in the first place; I can hardly back out now. And I can imagine it'll be all hands on deck over the next few days to get the orders out in time for Christmas.

'Good luck with all that,' Nick says, grinning. 'I've got a meeting tonight with a couple of colleagues to make sure we've dotted all the 'i's and crossed all our 't's for the morning.

'Oh, the joys of having a lawyer in the family,' Klaus says, shaking his head. 'You don't fancy coming down to the factory and lending a hand, then, Dad?'

'Knitting never was my thing, son.' Nick chuckles, standing up. 'I'll stick to what I'm good at.'

'Knitting?' Dad raises his eyebrows as he gets up. 'I'm looking forward to showing you around the factory, Nick. Show you how things are really done over there.'

'All in good time, Noel,' Nick replies, with a nod. 'For now I'll concentrate on getting that other place closed down. You just worry about replacing all those orders. Oh, and, don't forget, the press'll be very interested in what's been going on, too, so expect a few reporters over there tomorrow. I imagine you'll be kept mighty busy once word gets out, so be prepared for a long haul.'

'That's music to my ears,' Dad replies, slapping him on the back as they walk towards the door.

'I thought you might want to stay for dinner, Nick?' Mum looks quite disappointed as she follows them.

'Some other time, Eve, thanks. I really need to make a few calls before it gets too late. I'm sure Klaus won't mind sticking around, though, if you've made enough?'

'Of course.'

'See you later, Dad.' Klaus shouts up as they leave the room.

'Thanks so much,' I call out.

'Well, it looks like I'm staying to dinner,' Klaus says, smiling.

'That's not all you're going to get roped into if you're not careful,' I warn him. 'They'll need all the help they can get over at the factory, and we've already had a long day.' I can't help feeling a little guilty that Klaus will feel obliged to help, especially after everything he's done for us today.

'What? Spend the whole evening in your company? How will I ever cope?' His eyes twinkle as his lips near mine and suddenly his soft mouth is kissing me.

I close my eyes to savour the moment. It's only a quick kiss, as Mum and Dad will be back at any minute —but it's more than enough.

10

'TALK ABOUT SMELLY FEET!'

So much has changed in the week since I've been home. Merryville is back to the festive fantasyland we've all come to know and expect, with the streets, shops and houses dripping with tinsel and lights. As usual, the snow has hardly stopped falling since I arrived; making the whole town look like a perfect Christmas card scene, and the place has been awash with tourists for the past couple of days.

Klaus has been helping out in his family's toyshop, and I've been over at the factory trying desperately to get all the orders out on time.

'It looks like Jupiter Jumpers had lots more companies on their books that were relying on Christmas orders,' Dad tells us over breakfast. 'With the closure of their factory, those businesses are all hoping we can replace them as their suppliers.'

'That's good news, dear. At least you'll be able to recoup everything you lost from being closed down for the past few weeks.'

Dad nods, after taking a long swig of his tea. 'I think we've already caught up from that,' he says, smiling. 'My only concern is whether we'll be able to fulfil all their orders in time.'

'Especially with all the new companies that got in touch once they heard about us in the press,' I add, shaking my head with a yawn. 'You wouldn't have thought they'd still be putting in orders for festive jumpers this close to the big day, but it seems there's been a huge demand, for some reason.'

'It's the biggest trend of the year, according to the local paper,' Dad says, happily. 'It looks like our bit of publicity couldn't have come at a better time.'

'Everything always falls into place at Christmas,' Mum says, smiling. 'It's part of the magic of the season.'

'This year's certainly been different,' I admit, before taking another slice of toast from the rack. I know it's my fifth, but I have to keep my strength up somehow.

'How's Klaus getting on?' Mum asks, getting up to put more bread in the toaster. 'I'll bet it's really busy over at the shop.'

I nod, my mouth full, as usual. 'He's rushed off his

feet, but loving every minute,' I reply. 'The hotel's full as well as all the B&B's, and they've got coach loads visiting Merryville every day up until Christmas. All the publicity has certainly put us back on the map.'

'I think this has to be our busiest Christmas yet,' Dad agrees. 'And, talking of which, we'd better get going.'

'Finish your toast, love,' Mum encourages, putting the fresh rack of it on the table in front of him.

Dad doesn't need telling twice, and immediately reaches for the marmalade again.

'I'll go and get ready.' I stand up, stack up my dishes next to the sink and head upstairs to give Klaus another call.

I've really missed him over the past couple of days, but we've all been so busy there just hasn't been much time for socialising. We've been texting all the time, though, and calling whenever we're both free for a few minutes.

'I'm at the shop already,' he tells me, cheerfully. 'We're opening a bit early to try to alleviate the rush.'

'In that case, I won't keep you,' I promise. 'I just wanted to say hello, that's all. It seems like ages since we saw each other.'

Putting my hand across my tummy as I sit on the bed, I notice something sticky and roll my eyes at the patch of jam I've managed to spill there.

'You're right,' he says, with a tut. 'It's just so manic

right now. Feels like we've created a monster, just trying to help get everything back to normal, doesn't it?'

'It's good, though,' I admit, while rooting in my drawer for a clean jumper. 'Dad's really pleased that the factory's doing so well, and the whole atmosphere in the town's improved so much since we got all the decorations up.'

'Yeah, it's more of an excitement than a rush,' he agrees, with a little chuckle.

'Especially with the German Market tomorrow,' I add, placing the call on speakerphone while I haul off my sticky jumper.

'Grandad's so looking forward to it,' Klaus gushes. 'I think we're going to take it in turns to man the stall over there, as well as keep the shop going, so it'll be busy, but it should be great fun.'

'The factory's having a jumper stall, too,' I remind him. 'We might be able to work there at the same time, if we're lucky.'

Unfortunately, a bit if jam has got stuck in my hair and I have to pull hard to free the jumper, while biting my tongue at the pain to my head. Taking my phone, I rush into the bathroom to run some water over my sticky hair and hand.

'That'll be great.' He sounds genuinely excited. 'I was hoping we could meet up tonight, but I'm not sure there'll be time with the stall to set up and everything.'

'I'll be there tonight, anyhow, helping with ours, so I should see you anyhow,' I tell him, rubbing a towel over my hair.

A shout from downstairs makes me jump. 'I have to go. Sounds like we're leaving now. I'll chat to you in a bit.' I throw the towel into the bath and hurry back to the bedroom to find my clean jumper and a comb.

'Okay. Can't wait.'

I run downstairs, surprised to see Mum and Dad already in their coats waiting for me in the hallway.

'I was going to help with the dishes,' I tell Mum, feeling guilty.

'It's okay, I've done them.' She frowns at my hair which is all sticking up where I've pulled the jumper on over the wet patch, but doesn't mention it. 'Get your coat on, Dad's had a call from Bob Robinson. We need to get there as soon as we can.'

My stomach churns. 'Is everything okay?' I haul on my boots and grab my coat and bag before following them out the front door.

'We're not sure, yet. He's called a meeting with all the managers,' Mum replies as we pile into the Volvo.

'How did he sound, Dad?' I ask warily, strapping myself in before attempting to haul the comb through my damp hair.

'I'm not sure, to be honest, love. But he wants us all in asap, so it's got to be important.' Dad deftly manoeuvres the car off the snowy drive and sets off towards the town.

'Nick said they've shut down Jupiter's for the fore-seeable future,' I muse. 'While they continue their enquiries into the firm's business. I can't see them being a problem, can you?' Even the back of Dad's head looks a little tense.

'It's probably best not to speculate, love,' Mum says, turning back to give me a reassuring smile. 'We'll find out soon enough.'

I take the hint and concentrate on trying to sort out my hair. In desperation I take the little band I always keep wrapped around the end of my comb and tie it into a ponytail. Not quite the look I was going for today, but it'll do. Then I look out the window as we drive along, admiring all the lights and festive ornaments in the front gardens. I can't help smiling, thinking how different it all looked just over a week ago.

Dad goes straight into his meeting as soon as we arrive at the factory, and Mum goes to help in the admin office. I've been working on the factory floor for the past few days, checking samples of the work as the jumpers come zooming down the conveyor belt before being wrapped and stacked, ready for packing.

I must say, the array of bright colours makes me smile as I swipe off the odd item for a quality check. Jumpers for Joy definitely prides itself on the standard of their product, and I can see why people might have been disappointed to have received those cheap imitations Jupiter's were trying to pass off as ours. Even our colours are much more vivid, and the stitching's ten times better.

When the story got into the newspapers a few days ago, several people came forward to say that they'd been disappointed that the quality had gone downhill since Jupiter's 'took over' the company, and there was a general outrage about how misled the public had been by their company. It seems that our reputation is back intact and people are more than happy to support Jumpers for Joy again—which has led to some really late nights while we try to accommodate all the orders, but nobody's complaining.

Job security has been worth its weight in gold, and it seems the rest of the town has been assured that Merryville isn't going to let the same thing happen to any of our other businesses.

I can't wait for our morning break, when I catch up with Dad about his meeting. He's sitting in the staff canteen with Mum, looking very serious, and I suddenly feel a bit unnerved as I approach them.

'What happened?' I ask, putting my cup of tea on the table before taking the seat next to Mum.

'Drew Chapman's not happy,' Dad says, in a quiet voice. '

'Nothing new there, then,' I mutter.

'He's trying to claim that they were framed,' Dad

goes on. 'According to him they weren't trying to pass off their stock as ours at all. He's claiming that the patterns were *his* designs to start with—which has already been disproven, so there's nothing to worry about there—but that the labelling was an innocent mistake. Of course, Nick's pointed out that there was no reason for Jupiter's to have any of our labels in the first place, but Drew's trying to make out they were taken over there in error.'

I frown incredulously. 'What a load of hogwash!'

Mum nods. 'Of course it is, dear. Everyone knows that, but Drew's hoping to call a halt to our operation while the whole mess is sorted out.'

I gape at her. 'What? They can't close us down.'

'Shh,' Dad urges, and I quickly bite my lip.

'Sorry, Dad. But surely they can't do that? Not again? They've caused us enough disruption as it is. I can't believe they'd be allowed to stop our production because of their ridiculous claims.' My stomach roils with dread as I study my old man's face. He certainly looks unnerved by it all.

'Nick's fighting our corner, of course,' Dad replies, softly. 'We'll just have to wait and see what happens.' I can see by his glum expression that he's worried.

'What can we do to help, dear?' Mum asks, rubbing Dad's arm soothingly. 'You know we'll do whatever it takes.'

Dad smiles with a nod. 'I know, love.' He sighs. 'I

suppose the best thing is to keep going as fast as we can to get all these orders out just in case we have to close at the last minute. I'd hate to leave any of our retailers in the lurch just because of Chapman's shenanigans.'

I'm tempted to point out that we're already working as fast as the machinery will allow, but don't want to be a wet blanket, so I just nod. It's often the best way.

'That man's certainly got a lot to answer for,' Mum says with a tut.

'He's the type that always comes up smelling of roses, though,' Dad replies, grimacing.

'He won't be if he's wearing those suede loafers,' I muse, thinking aloud. 'Talk about smelly feet!'

It's good to see Dad looking much more relaxed as they both burst out laughing,

11

———

'HE'S NOT KNOWN AS 'THE LATE MAYOR OF MERRYVILLE' FOR NOTHING!'

We ended up working late into the night to get the majority of the orders finished in time, so we need to set up the market stall early this morning. Luckily, Klaus and his dad managed to set up theirs last night, so he's come over to help me for a bit, while his Grandma and Grandad finish cramming even more toys onto their stall.

The atmosphere feels like fireworks as everyone is getting ready for the grand opening. All of the stalls are decked out with tinsel and twinkling fairy lights, and the smells emanating from the food wagons is delicious. It's lovely to see some of the stallholders I recognise from previous years, as well as some new faces.

'Can I help you with that?' Klaus goes over to

where a lady is struggling with one of her tables, and he casually lifts it up. 'Where would you like it?'

'That's very kind of you,' she says, beaming at him. 'I was thinking at a sort of ninety degree angle to that one.'

Klaus obliges, and helps her put a beautiful glittery cloth over it, before coming back over to me.

'I think the jumpers are going over there,' I tell him, pointing to where a large lorry has just arrived behind one of the biggest stalls.

Dad must have arranged for a couple of guys to come down at the crack of dawn to set up the structure of the stall, as it has a metal frame which will be ideal for hanging the jumpers from. The tables are large enough to display plenty of the designs, though I'm pretty sure the ones with Christmas trees will be the most popular, being a German market, and all.

There are a couple of other stalls that aren't strictly German—like the candyfloss man, and the toffee-apple stall which also has a huge selection of fudge this year—but nobody minds. It's good to have some variety, and we've certainly got that by the bucket load today.

We go over to help unload the jumpers, glad to see that everyone is so happy and smiling around us. It's one of the friendliest places on earth, I'm sure of it, even though not everyone speaks fluent English.

· · ·

THE JUMPERS LOOK ABSOLUTELY stunning when we get them all unpacked and on display. We hang as many as we can, as it's the best way to show off the beautiful patterns, and the bright colours are really eye-catching. The tables are piled high with folded jumpers, carefully placed in size order—though I've a feeling they won't stay that way for long. Some have metallic threads running through them that glint in the sunlight, and we've got electricians fixing spotlights all around the stall, that will enhance the colours even more when it gets dark.

The market will go on late into the night, by which time most of us will be well-stuffed with all the delicious street food on offer and, no doubt, feeling the warming effects of the Glühwein.

People are already arriving as we add the finishing touches to the stall; a good helping of tinsel and fairy lights just to add to the atmosphere. Excited children gaze up at the different sights, while shoppers snap up the early-bird bargains.

'I'll need to get back to the toys,' Klaus announces once we're ready. 'Grandad's going back to the shop to help Dad, who opened up earlier. Apparently it's really busy over there already.'

'Thanks so much for your help.' We share a quick hug before I watch him make his way through the crowd towards his own stall. I really wish we could have worked together, but our families need to come first.

'Where's that mayor of ours got to now?' Mum moans, craning her neck to see over the shoppers. 'Trust him to be late on a day like this.'

Although some of the stallholders aren't too bothered, Dad always maintains that no one should be allowed to buy anything from the stall until the event has been officially opened. Otherwise, he reckons, there's no point in having an opening at all. I kind of get his point, but, honestly, our mayor would go to the opening of a crisp packet, so he's hardly a celebrity. And his tardiness is legendary. He's not known as 'the late mayor of Merryville' for nothing!

Someone you can rely on to attend these events, however, is our town crier. Standing at over seven-foot tall, he towers over proceedings with a huge smile and an extraordinarily loud voice. Mark Williams is a popular figure at all important occasions, and is easily distinguishable in his traditional 18th century costume, of red and gold coat, breeches, long black boots and black tricorne hat. The ring of his bell signals the arrival—at last—of the mayor.

Mayor Kevin Templeton is, by contrast, very small and unremarkable, with short brownish hair, wire-framed glasses and the most boring, monotone voice that ever sent you off to sleep. We can't see him from this distance, of course, and, despite the use of a megaphone, it's impossible to make out what he's actually saying, so we just wait for the Mexican wave of applause to reach us, indicating that we are finally open for business.

For the next couple of hours, we're inundated with customers, and there's hardly time to unpack the new stock before it's being sold. Despite how tired it made me, I'm really glad we made the effort to keep working until the early hours of this morning, as I'm sure we'd have run out of jumpers by coffee-time if not.

It's not just the amount of money we're making for the firm, it's also the good wishes and kind words of the customers that are making it all worthwhile. We knew that the locals were concerned for the future of Jumpers for Joy, as well as several other companies around here, but we're overwhelmed with the number of tourists who tell us that they can't come to Merryville without buying one of our famous designs. Old 'smelly-feet Chapman' would have caused a riot if he'd kept us out of business any longer, it seems. It's nice to know we're appreciated.

I'm a bit disappointed that Merryville Toys didn't get the stall right next to ours, but I know they can't be far away as I keep getting the distinct feeling that I'm being watched. I suppose it's not unusual, given the number of customers streaming to our stall, but this feels more intense than just shoppers waiting to be served. I wish I could see Klaus.

'I'll fetch more stock,' I yell to no one in particular, before diving onto the large lorry that's parked behind the stall.

Most of the staff are still serving, so I take the opportunity to text Klaus a quick message.

Hiya. Fancy meeting up for lunch in a bit? My break's at 1. It's manic over here. Where's your stall, btw? x

It's actually a bit warmer in the lorry, and I grab the first box I come to. I had thought that the whole lorry-load of jumpers might be a little ambitious for selling today, but I couldn't have been more wrong. Not only are people buying them in multiples, but we're also having lots of enquiries about the factory tours, which we hadn't really considered an option this year.

I've only just managed to drag the box to the edge of the lorry and jumped back out when my phone buzzes.

Hey, beautiful! Lunch sounds great! Grandma's gone back to the shop and I've got Dad working with me for a while. Really hectic here, too. We're over by the Lebkuchen stall with the German flag flying over it. Can't wait to see you. xx

Two kisses? I thought I was taking a chance putting one!

I can't stop smiling as I stuff the phone back into the pocket of my duffle coat and tear open the large box. My intention of lifting it onto the ground went out the window when I realised just how heavy it was, so I've decided to take the contents out piecemeal.

It's exhausting carrying piles of jumpers around to the stall, but it's got to be better than breaking my back. Besides, it's a good way to keep warm as the snow starts falling again. I've never known a Christmas in Merryville without snow.

By one o'clock I'm absolutely starving, and can't wait to catch up with Klaus. I'll bet there's a wonderful atmosphere over on their stall with all the children admiring the toys. It's what Christmas is all about, in my book.

Searching through the crowds, I notice there are several German flags flying, but I'm sure there's only one Lebkuchen stand. It takes a short while, but as soon as I smell gingerbread, I know I'm in the right area. Sure enough, iced gingerbread hearts are hung all around the Lebkuchen stall, which seems to have a constant stream of customers.

'I hadn't realised you were so far away from us,' I tell Klaus with a smile when I finally make my way around the back of his stall.

It's like a magical toyland with trains running along their tracks at the front, large wooden rocking horses at the back, and a myriad of different toys and dolls in between. I was right about the kids, too. Shiny faces are marvelling at the mechanical animals, and coos of admiration fill the air. In an age when computers and electronic games are so popular, it's heart-warming to see how fascinated the children are with these traditional toys.

I've never seen Nick smile so much, as he genuinely looks like he's enjoying serving the customers. He's great with the little children—I'm not sure why that surprised me so much—and beams as he demonstrates some clockwork cars.

'It's a shame we couldn't get stalls next to each other,' Klaus says, giving me a squeeze. 'We'll see you later, Dad.'

Nick gives us a quick wave of acknowledgement before continuing his conversation with the parents of a couple of sweet-looking twin boys.

'He looks happy,' I comment to Klaus as I link his arm and we head towards the food wagons.

'He is,' Klaus replies with a smile. 'I think he's really in his element today. He started off in the shop this morning, and said the atmosphere over there was electric. Now he's come to help me he hasn't stopped grinning. He says it reminds him of being a kid again.'

'That's what Christmas is all about,' I say, squeezing his arm a little tighter.

He chuckles. 'I think you're right. How about a hot dog? They've got bratwurst over there if you fancy it?'

'I can't stay too long, I'm afraid. Our stall's really busy and I need to make sure Mum gets a proper break,' I tell him as he hands me a huge bratwurst hot dog topped with sauerkraut and red onion.

'I know. In fact, I'd best take one of these back for Dad,' Klaus says with a nod, before ordering an extra portion.

'I'm surprised your dad's got time for working here today, what with everything else he's got going on with the case,' I comment.

'Oh, he's got it all in hand. Besides, he's got a couple of his associates working on it, too,' Klaus assures me. 'And to be honest, I don't think he'd miss this for the world, but he'd never admit it.'

We take a look around a few stalls while eating our lunch. They've got everything you could possibly want for Christmas here, from decorations to gifts and food.

'Oh look, these are so pretty,' I say, picking up a little silver bracelet with different coloured stones hanging from it.

'Try it on,' the lady behind the stall urges.

'Good idea,' Klaus urges with a smile. 'I'll bet it'll look lovely on you.'

After pulling the sleeve of my coat up a little to expose my wrist, I quickly fasten the little lobster claw and admire the lovely colours.

'We'll take it,' Klaus tells the lady, putting down the bag with his Dad's lunch in and pulling his wallet from his pocket.

'Oh Klaus! I wasn't hinting—'

'I know you weren't,' he assures me with a smile. 'I wanted to get you something you'd like, and I could see how much you were admiring it. Call it a Christmas present.' He winks to me, making my insides melt, and I look back at the beautiful gift.

'I'll never want to take it off,' I tell him once he's paid and we walk away from the stall. 'Thank you so much.'

'My pleasure,' he assures me, before bending down to give me a chaste kiss on the lips. 'Happy Christmas.'

I smile back at him. 'D'you know, I honestly think it will be.'

12

**'...NICK SAINT. SAINT NICK. HAS
ANYONE EVER TOLD YOU THAT
YOUR NAME'S...?'**

We stop to buy some mince pies at a stall along the way.

'Mum'll love these,' I say, looking at the array in front of us. Who knew there were so many variations?

I spy my favourites and smile at the man behind the counter, who's dressed in a very smart, woolly coat, with a red and white 'Santa' hat perched rather incongruously on his bald head. 'I'll take half a dozen of the iced ones, please.'

Klaus shakes his head beside me. '*Iced* mince pies? Really?'

I stare at him in surprise. 'They're the best,' I inform him.

'I'll take a box of the traditional ones, please,' Klaus tells the man, before rolling his eyes at me.

'What's not traditional about icing?' I gape at him incredulously. 'You always have icing at Christmas. It's everywhere.'

'Not on mince pies,' Klaus says, firmly. 'Mince pies are mince pies. Icing goes on cake.'

'You sound like my dad,' I tell him.

'Your dad's a sensible man,' Klaus replies with a nod, taking the boxes from the man. 'You should listen to him.'

WHEN WE RETURN to the toy stall, we're surprised to see Kevin Templeton, our town mayor, talking animatedly with Nick.

'Ah, there you are.' Nick turns with a smile as we arrive. 'We were just discussing the Christmas party. Kevin was hoping we could provide the gifts for the children again this year.'

'Of course,' Klaus replies, handing his dad his lunch. 'We'd be glad to.'

'Could you store them until Christmas Eve?' the mayor asks. Then he lowers his voice. 'I've spoken to Santa, who's happy to make his appearance and hand them out.'

Nick nods. 'No problem. Just let us know how many and the ages and we'll get it all organised. I'm sure I know a couple of little elves who won't mind helping with the wrapping.' He looks pointedly at me and Klaus, and we just nod back as 'elvishly' as we can.

'Good. That's settled, then.' Kevin shakes Nick's free hand. 'Thanks for that, Nick. You're a saint. Ha—see what I did there? Nick Saint. Saint Nick. Has anyone ever told you that your name's…?'

Nick raises his eyebrows. 'No. I can't say I've ever noticed.' His sarcasm is lost on the mayor, who guffaws at his own joke as he leaves the stall in a fit of hysterics. We can hear him repeating it to unsuspecting shoppers on his way into the crowd.

Nick just rolls his eyes.

The Merryville Christmas Party is the highlight of the whole season and it's such a relief to hear it's going ahead this year. We have a huge street party in the square, with long tables laid out for the local children with traditional party food, including lots of festive treats. At the same time there is a large marquee set up as the beer tent, where the adults congregate for a drink and more seasonal nibbles. It's a fantastic event, where everyone takes turns in supervising the children and having fun.

Fancy dress is optional, and we always have adults dressed up as different well-known characters, as well as jugglers, magicians, and the like to entertain everyone.

The event culminates at seven o'clock with a firework display for the children and a visit from Santa before they go home. Then it's the adults' time to have some fun. We all help clear up, then lay down a dance floor and enjoy some dancing with live music and often the odd comedian or two—and we really have had some rather 'odd' comedians over the years. Everyone laughs anyway, probably because by then we're all enjoying a well-earned drink. It's a fantastic occasion for everyone, and one of the many attractions that have tourists flocking to spend Christmas in Merryville year after year.

'Your gran and I are swapping again this afternoon,' Nick announces, tucking into his hotdog. 'Grandad will need to start organising all the presents for the party, so I'll have to mind the shop.' He points to a folded up chair in the corner behind the stall. 'Make sure your gran gets to sit down and take it easy; she'll be getting tired with everything that's going on, but she still wants to help.'

Klaus nods. 'Don't worry, Dad. I'll keep an eye on her.'

'Thanks, son. Those two aren't getting any younger, though they'll never admit it.'

'I'd better get back to work, too,' I say, a little ruefully. I'd love to spend the rest of the day here with Klaus and all these excited children.

I'm surprised when Klaus turns and gives me a big hug, right in front of his dad. 'Have fun,' he mutters into my ear.

'You too. And thanks again for this.' I touch my bracelet, smiling.

'You're welcome. D'you want me to walk you back to your stall?'

It's really kind of him to offer—and I'd really love it if he would—but I can see how many eager faces are looking up at him, vying for his attention, and I simply can't deny them that.

'No, it's fine. I'll text you later.' I squeeze his arm. 'Looks like you've got your work cut out for you here.'

Klaus gives me a soft kiss on the cheek before I turn and leave. I can feel the heat rising in my face, and I'm really touched that Klaus didn't mind showing his affection in front of his dad. Most guys would run a mile rather than do that. But then, I've come to realise, Klaus isn't like other guys.

Mum's really pleased when I tell her about the Christmas Party. She's usually very proactive with the organisation of it, rallying all her WI friends to help with the food and decorations, while the people on the town council are responsible for booking the marquee, bars and entertainment.

Although Dad's usually too busy with the factory, a group of the men usually take care of all the heavy lifting on the day, with the chairs and tables, as well as helping set up the marquee and a small stage for the musicians and acts. Dad joins us as soon as the factory closes, as do all the workers, though they only employ a skeleton staff on Christmas Eve, and always shut early.

'It really seems like we're going to have a traditional Merryville Christmas after all,' she says with a beaming smile.

'And Klaus sounded quite sure that his dad has everything under control with that hiccup at the factory,' I add.

'Let's hope so, love.'

Dad comes to join us for an hour in the afternoon, looking much more relaxed than he did yesterday. 'It's all systems go at the factory,' he tells us. 'We've even had more orders in today from a couple of firms we haven't dealt with before. They want us to send out their stock on Christmas Eve, ready for their Boxing Day Sales.'

'They're not planning to sell our lovely designs at knockdown prices, are they?' Mum raises her eyebrows, while straightening up a pile of jumpers on the stall in front of her.

'No, dear, of course not. It's all sprats to catch mackerel.' Dad shakes his head. 'They're hoping to woo customers in with the sale items, and then upsell the new jumpers while they're there. They're going for the element of surprise, having something totally new to offer their shoppers.'

Mum nods. 'Oh, I see.'

'You've got to admit it's a good idea,' I comment.

'It's a *very* good idea,' Dad agrees. 'But it also makes more work for us right on Christmas. And this year of all years is proving to be quite a challenge, I can tell you.'

I frown. 'You do think we can do it all though, right, Dad? I mean, we've got all the staff back in and no one's complaining about the overtime after the past couple of weeks they've just had.'

Dad nods. 'We think we can just about make it,' he assures me. 'We really don't want to bite off more than we can chew, but looking forward we desperately need these new retailers on board. We can't afford to let anyone down.'

'We won't.' *I think Klaus's optimism really is rubbing off on me.*

Dad smiles. 'That's the spirit.'

'The *Christmas* spirit,' Mum pipes up, beaming. 'Anything's possible at Christmas.'

It looks like this optimism-thing's contagious!

Dad's a bit more reserved than me and Mum, I notice, although he's very polite and charming with the customers. I can see why he usually works in an office, behind the scenes. Oddly enough, though, I note how the shoppers seem drawn to him in favour of some of the other staff who are shouting at the tops of their voices, always touting for more custom even when they're in the middle of serving someone. I suppose it takes all sorts, but it's interesting to see just how many jumpers Dad is selling.

'I need to get back shortly,' Dad announces after a while.

'Chris bought us some mince pies. At least have one before you go,' Mum urges, opening the box.

Dad sniffs. 'They've got icing on.'

'They're very nice,' Mum insists.

'I think I'll pass, thanks.' Dad shakes his head.

I can see that Dad and Klaus are going to get along.

'All the more for us.' I reach over and pull one out before Mum has time to close the box. 'Mmm,' I moan loudly after taking the first bite. 'Delicious. You don't know what you're missing.'

Dad rolls his eyes. 'I'll take that chance, thanks love. I appreciate the gesture, though.' He leans over and kisses the top of my head before giving Mum a big hug.

'Don't work too hard,' Mum calls after him as he leaves us.

'He only said he had to get back—nothing about working when he gets there,' I remind her with a grin.

The rest of the afternoon sails by with a constant stream of customers. As soon as evening falls the lights become more vivid and the atmosphere changes slightly. Although there are still hordes of shoppers, it doesn't seem quite so manic, somehow.

The fair's started up over in the square, so people are starting to drift over there, and the food stands suddenly become even more popular.

'We've sold nearly the whole lorry-load today,' Mum says with a smile. 'You're dad'll be pleased.'

I look at the last couple of unopened boxes in the far corner of the lorry. 'Let's get them all sold,' I say, a sudden determination rising to the fore.

'D'you think we can?' One of the ladies from the factory calls over, frowning. 'It's thinning out a bit now, dear. I think you'll find people are more interested in eating and drinking than buying jumpers.'

'Of course.' I dive into the lorry and shuffle the boxes to the edge. 'We've sold thousands already; I'm sure we can get through a few hundred more before we close.'

'We'll have to be here all night to shift that lot,' one of the men grumbles, rather unhelpfully to my mind.

'If we all pull together and really work at it I reckon we can do it,' I point out, giving him a hard stare that he clearly doesn't notice.

'We've still got all this to sell first, though.' A blonde girl with lots of makeup waves her hand over the stall. She might be pretty, but her tone is downright condescending.

Despite all the answers I want to give her, I settle for biting my tongue and smiling sweetly.

One of her friends laughs, rather derisively. 'What

do you expect, Melanie? She doesn't even work at the factory, how would she know how hard it is to sell anything?'

Okay, now the gloves are off!

'You don't sell them at the factory; you press the buttons on the machines that make them,' I point out. 'And, as I work in advertising, I think I've got a pretty good idea how to sell, thank you very much.' I swallow hard before adding, 'and, for your information, I worked at the factory before you even joined the staff.'

Melanie whispers something to her and the girl just scowls at me.

'Come on, we're wasting time,' Mum chirps up, springing into action before things turn nasty. 'If we're going to get all this sold today we need to get on with it. 'Melanie, why don't you and the girls pile up those jumpers so we can fit more on? Patrick, get Rob to help you bring those boxes over, will you? We'll stack on as much as we can. Shoppers like to see lots of stock. It gives them more choice.'

'If we can get the larger sizes hanging up, it'll give us more room for the smaller ones on the tables,' I suggest.

'Good idea. Give me a hand to lift down some of those kids' ones, will you?' Mum thrusts one of the telescopic boat hooks into my hand, and we set about removing the smaller jumpers for some of the girls to fold and put on the table.

I feel quite excited as we hook up the larger jumpers, and it's a thrill to see the bottom of the first box once we've emptied it. I'm more determined than ever to do well today—if only to prove Melanie and her friends wrong.

'Do you want the last box opened?' Patrick calls over as Mum and I fix the jumpers to the racking.

Mum looks at the display a little doubtfully. 'I'm not sure we'll have room.'

'We will have once these have all sold,' I remind her. I call over to Patrick. 'Yes, please. Open the box but leave it behind the stall. We can put them out as soon as we've sold a few of these.'

Mum smiles. 'You're feeling very positive.'

I nod. 'When you consider everything else we've accomplished this past week, selling a few jumpers should be a doddle.'

'You're right, love. You've worked wonders since you got home.'

'*We've* worked wonders, Mum. It's a team effort, don't forget.'

'Let's just hope everyone appreciates it,' Mum says in a voice loud enough for the girls to hear.

I shudder. It's not that cold, but I get the feeling I'm being watched again, and this time I know it can't be Klaus. Maybe it's Melanie's eyes boring into my back…

13

'PEOPLE WHO THINK ALOUD SHOULDN'T BE ALLOWED TO THINK,'

I could really get used to this 'being right' thing. The fair's in full swing as we throw the last of the empty boxes in to the back of the lorry.

Melanie and her friends went home an hour or so ago so, unfortunately, I don't get to see the delight on their faces when they realise we *did* manage to sell every last one of the jumpers.

A couple of other girls, Lucy and Millie, and I took some of the jumpers into the crowd and actually approached people to buy them. It was another bright idea I'd picked up on my advertising course—though I wasn't expecting it to work quite as well as it did. It seemed several people had admired our jumpers from a distance but didn't have the energy to walk all the way to our stall, so we were actually doing them a huge favour. Once we realised this, we went further towards the fair and made loads more sales. We also looked like walking adverts for the stall, and lots of people went to check it out after seeing us in the crowds, according to Mum. It's a tactic I'll definitely use again.

'Well, I could certainly do with a good rest after today,' Mum says with sigh, as the clanging of metal bars indicates that the men are already disassembling the stall.

'We need to meet up tomorrow, Eve,' her friend calls over to her. 'The WI needs to discuss arrangements for the party.'

It's Amanda Jones, the chairperson of the aforementioned committee. She's a lovely lady, but can be very forthright when she needs to get something done. It seems this is one of those occasions.

'Yes, of course.' Mum goes over to her, smiling, though she's clearly shattered.

'I'll get hold of Mrs. Blackenbury first thing and see what she's got in mind. I'm assuming it'll be the usual. Then we can meet up and discuss who's making what.'

'Great idea.' Mum's still smiling, bless her!

'I have to admit, we were all wondering if the party was going to go ahead this year,' Amanda lowers her voice a little. 'What with everything that's been going on, and all.'

'It's Christmas,' Mum replies, matter-of-factly.

'You're right.' Amanda looks thoughtful. 'A time for miracles.' She nods.

'A time for everyone to pull together,' Mum replies.

KLAUS COMES over to see me just before we leave.

'I need to take my Grandma back,' he says, a little apologetically.

I nod. 'I'll bet she's shattered by now; it's been a long day.'

'I'm sorry. I was hoping we could go to the fair or something.' He puts an arm around me.

'Don't worry. I'm ready for my bed now, too. I've hardly sat down all day.'

'Are you working at the factory tomorrow?' he asks.

'Just for a few hours. Dad's agreed to let everyone who worked on here today get a bit of a lie-in in the morning.' I try to stifle a yawn but fail miserably. 'Sorry. I think all the fresh air's made me tired.'

'Not to mention the Glühwein,' Mum cuts in.

Klaus grins. 'I couldn't drink any as I'm driving Dad's car back, but I've picked up a few bottles to enjoy once I'm home.'

'Very sensible.' Mum nods approvingly.

'Hey, *I'm* not driving tonight,' I point out.

It's no good, she's already moved on as Dad's coming down the road.

'I enjoyed today but I wish we'd been able to see more of each other,' Klaus says, turning to face me, with both arms around my waist.

'Me, too. I was hoping we'd have stalls next to each other or something.'

'I know you're busy tomorrow, but what about the day after? I'd like to show you around the shop and workshop.' He winks. 'And if you're really good I'll let you know where Santa hides all the presents for the good children before Christmas Eve.'

I narrow my eyes at him with a smile. 'Okay, Santa. Define 'good'.'

He bursts out laughing. 'Well now...'

'Time to go,' Dad calls over from where he's been chatting with Mum and the guys taking down the stall.

I roll my eyes. 'Looks like we're off,' I tell Klaus. 'But I'd love to come and see your shop and everything.'

He wraps me in a warm hug. 'We'll work it all out tomorrow.' He kisses me lightly on the lips before letting me go. 'Text me when you get home, just to let me know you're safe.'

I nod, while my heart melts a little bit more.

ALTHOUGH IT'S HORRENDOUSLY BUSY, the atmosphere in the factory today is much lighter than I expected. Everyone was pleasantly surprised at how much we managed to sell yesterday—no one expected us to sell the whole lorry-full.

It's been a bit of a double-edged sword, however, as

it's meant we have to make even more stock to fulfil all the Christmas orders, and we've only got three more days.

The machines are churning out jumpers like they're going out of fashion—*heaven forbid!*—and the packing area, where I'm working for a change, is totally manic. I'm currently labelling up boxes for different customers, which is no mean feat when the items coming off the production line aren't in the order I'd like them to be.

'That's the last of Poulson's Pullovers,' I tell Dad when he comes in to check on us.

'Great. I'll get Dave to get the lorry down and we'll get it out this afternoon,' Dad says, nodding. I can tell he's relieved to get that one out of the way. Frank Poulson isn't just a friend, he's also our best customer, and has been a catalyst in getting all our other regulars to come back to us—not that they realised they'd ever left us in the first place, mind you.

'We'll get them all moved over to the loading bay so they're ready to go,' I promise.

Dad nods with a smile. Then he leans into me and says in a low voice 'Nick's been in touch. The police are expected to start making arrests any day now. I'll be surprised if Jupiter Jumpers ever opens its doors again.'

I beam at him, before giving him a big hug. 'That's great news, Dad. We can put this all behind us by Christmas and get back to normal.'

'Normal?' He gives me an incredulous look. 'Have you seen how many new clients we've got signed up for next year? We won't know what's hit us when we have to start on their orders. We're talking about taking on more staff to help out.'

'Even better.' I squeeze him again with a giggle. 'Not only are we back in business, but we're doing better than ever!'

'Bob's suggested we might see if Jupiter's factory's available in the New Year so we can expand.' Dad chuckles.

'What? We can't possibly make our lovely designs over in that place,' I protest. 'It's the homely feel around here that puts the love into our jumpers. They just wouldn't feel the same if they were made in a place like that.'

'You've got a good point there, love.' He nods, raising his eyebrows. 'I think I'll use that as part of the argument against it if it comes up again. To be honest, I hope he was just thinking aloud.'

'People who think aloud shouldn't be allowed to think,' I point out. 'Not if they're thinking up such rubbish ideas as that, anyway.'

We both laugh, and it's great to see Dad looking so relaxed and happy. He loves his job here and I really couldn't imagine him doing anything else. Mum isn't working today, as she was so tired after yesterday, and I've been promised at least a half-day off tomorrow.

'I've managed to convince Yasmine Fothergill and Morgan Baines to send us some of their staff to help out, by the way,' Dad says, triumphantly. 'We really don't need much advertising and marketing at the moment; we've got enough work to keep us going for a while, and it's crucial that we get these orders fulfilled on time.'

'Does Yasmine still work here?' I ask in surprise. 'I haven't seen her since I've been back, but then, I've been over this end most of the time, haven't I?'

'She does,' Dad informs me with a beam. 'And she was very impressed at how you managed to organise all the publicity for the town and the market and so forth. She knows you're up to your eyes at the moment, but she said to go see her when you have time. Said she'd like to have a chat.'

My stomach churns with excitement. Yasmine Fothergill is the head of advertising here at the company and she's absolutely brilliant at her job. She's also a really nice lady, and has always taken an interest in my career.

I thought about asking her for a job here once, but really wanted to stand on my own two feet. That's why I was so pleased to get the position over in Greenchurch, but it wasn't quite what I expected. I daren't tell Mum and Dad how miserable I am over there as they're so proud of me, but I secretly wish I'd never left home. Not that I'd want to live with my parents forever, but I just love Merryville and everyone in it—well, most people, anyway; I'm not so keen on that Melanie-girl from last night, to be honest. Nor her friend, come to think of it.

'I'll pop over when I get my break,' I tell Dad.

He nods. 'You do that.'

He's still smiling when he leaves me, which is always a good sign, I reckon. My mind's racing. I've actually managed to impress Yasmine Fothergill! Who would have believed it? My stomach's all jittery with nerves, and I have to concentrate hard on what I'm doing to stop my hopes running away with me. Stay focused, Chris. Unfortunately, sliding boxes onto a trolley to take them over to the loading area doesn't take too much brain-power and I can't stop thinking about Yasmine.

I end up working through until lunchtime, thanks to a mix up with some of the boxes—not my fault, I hasten to add. By the time one o'clock comes around I'm starving.

I've brought some sandwiches for my lunch, so I quickly wolf them down before taking the lift up to the offices. The last thing I want is for my stomach to start rumbling when I'm trying to impress Yasmine Fothergill.

'Chris, how nice to see you again.' She stands up when she sees me, and I suddenly feel quite nervous. I run my fingers over the smooth stones of the bracelet

Klaus bought me yesterday, and find it surprisingly calming.

Yasmine is a very successful woman, with the designer clothes to prove it. I've always aspired to be like her—Chanel bag included, and she's part of the reason I pursued a career in advertising in the first place.

'I've been helping out down in the factory,' I tell her. *As if she didn't know!* 'It's been all hands to the pump trying to get all the orders out on time.'

She nods, indicating for me to take the chair opposite her. Seeing her in her gorgeous shift dress with matching jacket and Louboutins makes me wish I'd dressed a bit smarter before coming to see her. We only wear casual clothes on the factory floor as we have overalls over the top anyhow, to stop anything getting caught in the machinery. Of course, I removed mine before coming up here, but I'm only in jeans and a jumper. Again I'd raided my stash of seasonal woollies this morning, but I'm starting to regret the large reindeer with googly eyes that's now staring at the very smart lady in front of me.

'Your father informed me that you're still working over in Greenchurch,' she goes on, with a smile. 'How are you finding it?'

I take a deep breath. How do I answer that one? If I tell her I love it, she'll never offer me a job here. But if I say I hate it she might think I'm no good at advertising. Why is everything so complicated?

'Greenchurch is a lovely little town,' I begin, hoping she can't sense my hesitance.

Her puzzled expression tells me she can. 'Do you enjoy advertising?' she asks, sitting back in her chair a little. I'm not sure if that's a sign that she's relaxed and enjoying our conversation—it'd be good if at least one of us was—or if she's given up on me and is just making herself comfy.

'Yes. I love writing press releases and contacting the media,' I tell her, sitting forward. Now this is something I can talk about! 'I've actually made some good contacts with some of the national papers, and I've been in touch with someone at the BBC several times, too. And of course local radio stations and papers.'

She smiles, sitting forward again. 'That's good. I know you did a wonderful job getting Merryville back on the map—and we're all really grateful for your help in getting the factory back on track, of course.'

Melanie isn't!

'I couldn't bear the thought of Merryville not celebrating Christmas,' I admit. 'Honestly, it would have been tragic. Not to mention what it would have done to local trade. I was afraid that if people stopped coming even for just a year we'd undo so much of the work we've done previously to make Merryville the place to be at this time of year.

'People make other arrangements, and then those arrangements become their norm, don't they? And I'm sure the tourists would feel let down by us and possibly boycott us in future, anyway. It would ruin everything; our reputation, our trade, the lot.' I'm aware that my voice has become a little louder and I've certainly been talking faster as I'm so passionate about the subject, but Yasmine doesn't seem to mind.

She nods. 'I agree. We were all devastated when they announced we'd have to close the factory, but then cancelling Christmas on top of that was just another nail in Merryville's coffin. Several of us tried to convince the local council to trade as normal over the festive period, but there was so much uncertainty about the future they decided it was for the best. They kept reiterating that it was only for one year, but, as you said, we might never have resurrected our standing if they'd gone through with it.'

A lady I vaguely recognise suddenly arrives with a tray of tea and biscuits. Yasmine looks up with a smile. 'Thank you, Claire.'

I'm delighted to see that they're not just any old biscuits, either. These are Fox's with the thick chocolatey coating I love so much. We only have them for very special occasions in our house, and even then Mum always mixes them up with a couple of more mundane varieties so I can't just scoff all the nice ones. I'm beginning to like Yasmine even more, and I could just about kiss her when she says the magic words; 'help yourself.'

'What are the company like to work for?' *She just had to go and spoil it, didn't she?* 'Wheeler, Rouse and Marshall, isn't it?'

Damn! She knows them. I'll bet she's best friends with Jennifer Marshall, too, the woman who's made my life hell for the past couple of years! This is just getting worse!

'They're a very large company with lots of clients on their books,' I begin, eyeing another chocolate biscuit on the plate in front of me. 'They're very successful and good at what they do.'

Yasmine nods. 'Yes, they've got a good reputation for getting results.'

'Yes.' I'm not really sure what else to say, in all honesty. I fidget a little uncomfortably.

'I've heard it's not exactly the friendliest place to work, though.' She leans forward with a little knowing smile.

Hallelujah!

'You're right,' I admit with a huge sigh. 'Some of the people there are really horrid.' *I daren't name names, of course.*

'Are all the partners still working there?' She asks, before taking a sip of her tea.

I nod. 'Philip Rouse is supposed to be a sleeping partner, but we see more of him than we do Joan

Wheeler. But I've met them all. Jennifer Marshall is the one I have more to do with on a day-to-day basis.'

'And how do you find her?'

'Erm...' I suddenly take a deep interest in my tea, and take a big gulp to buy myself some thinking time.

'I never liked her much,' Yasmine offers.

I stare at her. 'You know her?'

She nods. 'I worked there for a short while after I graduated,' she reveals. 'To be honest, Jennifer made my life a misery so I left. I'm amazed you've managed to stick it out so long. How is she with you?'

'Jennifer Marshall's a grade 'A' bitch,' I announce. *Remember that bit about not naming names...?*

'I'm so glad it's not just me.' Yasmine bursts out laughing and I follow suit as relief washes over me. 'Honestly, I thought it was just me she had it in for,' she goes on.

'Oh no, it's everyone,' I tell her. 'Everyone moans about her but there's nothing anyone can do. She owns the company, after all. No one's going to make a complaint about the boss, are they?'

'That's the trouble,' Yasmine agrees with a grimace. 'These people in power are untouchable. Still, once people know about them it's their personal reputation that's damaged, and that's something you can't rectify.'

I frown, trying to figure out what she's telling me.

'It's a small world,' she explains. 'Everyone knows everyone else in the advertising business—or if they don't know them, they know *of* them. Word gets around. And mud sticks. Everyone in the know is aware of how they treat their staff in that place. Pretty soon word will leak out to the clients, and no one wants to work with a bully, no matter how good they are.' She gives me a secretive smile. 'She'll get her comeuppance, don't you worry.'

I feel a strange calmness overtake me. I think the worse thing about being in any bad situation is the feeling of hopelessness. Knowing you can't do a damn thing about it. Suddenly it feels like there is hope, after all.

Yasmine relaxes into her seat again. 'So, how much longer are you planning to stick it out over there?'

'Only until I get a better offer.' The words tumble out of my mouth and I'm only glad my third chocolate biscuit doesn't follow them. I gulp, realising what I've just said.

Yasmine beams. 'Well, in that case I'd better get my skates on before someone else snaps you up.'

My jaw just about hit the floor, making me glad I've already swallowed the last of that biscuit.

'I don't know that I'm actually 'snapping-up' mater-ial,' I admit.

Yasmine laughs. 'Modest with it, I see.' She leans forward again. 'It's common knowledge that it was *you* who put Merryville back on the map this year, and that you were a catalyst in getting this place back up and running again. You're a good catch, I assure you.'

I suppose I'd never even thought of it like that.

'So, how would you feel about working here? I mean, with your dad being here, and all? Would that be a problem?' She raises her eyebrows.

'No. Of course not. I get on great with my dad, and we don't exactly work in the same circles do we? I mean... I'd love to work here.'

'Great. I need someone with your drive and ambition. Now, at the moment I've had to relinquish most of my staff to help downstairs, but after Christmas we'll be getting back to normal again. How would you like to join the team? We work closely with Morgan over in Marketing, too, so you'd be doing some of that, but primarily I want you in Advertising. How does that sound?'

'Brilliant.' I swallow hard, trying to take it all in. This is a dream come true. 'I'd love to.'

She beams again. 'Good to hear. How much notice do you need to give your current employer?'

'A month.' The thought gives me a sinking feeling in my stomach again.

'That's okay. You can tender your notice while you're on holiday, can't you? I mean, the firm's still open until Christmas Eve, isn't it?'

'Yes.' I hadn't thought of that.

'Plus you'll need some time to move out of your

accommodation in Greenchurch. And I'm guessing there would be some people you'd want to say goodbye to over there?' She smiles.

'Of course.' I suddenly feel much better.

'So we can make your start whenever you want after your notice period is over,' she says, standing up. 'I'll talk to you again and we'll set something up. In the meantime, welcome aboard. Oh, and I guarantee your wages will be much better than whatever they're paying you.'

I stand up, too, though my legs are a little wobbly with all the excitement. We shake hands, though it's much warmer than a usual business handshake.

'I'm looking forward to working with you, Chris,' she says with another of her beaming smiles.

'I can't wait to start,' I admit.

'We'll sort out the formalities after Christmas when everything's a bit calmer,' she promises as I head for the door. 'Oh, and take these with you for your coffee break.' She quickly wraps the last of the biscuits in a napkin. 'I won't eat them and they'll only go to waste.'

I take them from her, barely refraining from giving her a hug. I think I'm really going to love my new boss!

14

'SOMETIMES I THINK SHE'S TOO SENSIBLE FOR MY OWN GOOD!'

Mum and Dad were so pleased when I told them about my new job, that Dad's given me the whole day off today. Of course, he might have changed his mind when I mentioned it meant I'd be moving back home, at least for a bit, but luckily he's a man of his word and knew better than to back out of an agreement.

I'm really looking forward to actually spending a whole day with Klaus, and can't wait to see around the shop and workshop. It's been years since I visited Merryville Toys, and, even then, I never got to see behind the scenes.

I'm certainly not disappointed when the taxi pulls up in front of the shop, and gasp as I get out of the car into the thick snow. It's like a scene from a fairytale with the whole building smothered in twinkling lights, and the snow piled up on the roof and windowsills. More lights are shining from inside and the chatter of excited children can be heard even before I open the door.

The shop is double-fronted, with large, well-decorated bow windows either side of the entrance. A train is running around the track in one of them, with a whole scene surrounding it including houses, people and numerous animals. The other side shows a large open dolls house complete with furniture, dolls and a really pretty garden, with a paddock and a stable with horses in one corner. It really is magical and I can imagine any child wishing for these toys under their tree on Christmas day.

A bell tinkles as I open the door and warmth welcomes me inside. Soft festive music is playing in the background, but most of the noise comes from the chattering of delighted children.

Klaus beams at me from behind the counter where his dad and grandad are chatting with a group of happy-looking customers.

'Hey, I'm so glad you could make it,' Klaus says, whizzing over to give me a big hug.

'I couldn't wait. And I've got some news for you,' I say, relishing his warmth. I hadn't wanted to tell him over the phone last night so he doesn't know yet about the job. I've been dying to tell him in person, but it can wait until we're alone.

'Now I'm intrigued,' he admits, grinning.

A comforting feeling envelopes me as I look around the shop. 'It's been yonks since I came in here,' I tell him, going over to look at a pretty boxed doll on the shelf nearby. 'I always wanted one of these.'

'The place has certainly been here a long time,' Klaus says, looking around. 'But we've always looked after it and it's looked after us.' He smiles. 'It's a happy place.'

I nod. 'Yeah, it is.'

A couple of young children charge past us, playing with plastic swords, and Klaus swiftly puts a protective arm around me.

'We've got more modern toys and games through there,' he says, pointing to an archway I hadn't noticed before. 'Dad had this bit added on a couple of years ago to cater for the less-traditional customers.'

The building is a large, log cabin with a wooden interior that lends itself beautifully to traditional handmade toys. Through the archway, however, is an extension of the natural-looking décor, but with brighter lighting and cabinets containing computers and consoles. The dark brown carpet that runs through the shop continues in here, but has the added feature of a large orange and yellow rug in the centre of the floor. I can certainly see how this might appeal to slightly older children who are looking for more modern forms of entertainment.

'This is lovely,' I enthuse, admiring the tasteful décor.

'Grandad's not so keen.' Klaus grimaces, and I remember him telling me about it in the taxi when we first met. 'But Dad's happy with it, and the manager loves it in here.'

I look around, expecting to see someone behind the counter, but we're alone.

'He's on holiday,' Klaus explains, as though reading my mind again. 'Neal's family are from Scotland, so he wanted to go home for Christmas. As we were all coming home anyway, it made sense for us to look after the place so he could take a well-earned rest.'

'That was good of you.' I'm not used to bosses being so kind, but I've got a feeling I'm about to experience it in my new job.

'It's important to look after your staff,' Klaus states. Then he leans in a little closer. 'Besides, we sell much more of the traditional stuff when Grandad's here. He makes a lot of it himself, too, which people love to see.'

'He's not here all the time, then, your Grandad?'

Klaus shakes his head. 'No. Grandma and Grandad live up north. They always come down for Christmas, though—which is when most people are looking for more traditional toys, anyway.'

I nod. It makes sense. 'It's a shame in a way, though, as I'd love to see more of your grandparents.'

'They'll be here until just after New Year,' he tells me with a smile.

'So will *you* be running this place or the manager?' I ask, going over to examine some laptops in a cabinet on the wall.

'I'm hoping he'll be staying on when I take over,' Klaus says. 'We get along fine, but I know it's going to be a bit odd for him when I'm here all the time. He's used to being here on his own, with just a part-timer to keep an eye on the other side when it's busier. I'm hoping to make it busy all the time so we can keep them both on and I can make a better go of it, to be honest.'

I frown, turning to face him. 'You don't think he's doing a great job, then?'

Klaus grimaces. 'It's not that. It's just.... '

'What?' I'm not sure it's any of my business, but I can't help feeling intrigued.

'Come on, I'll show you the workshop,' he says, leading me to a door at the very back of the shop. He unlocks it and opens the door to reveal a large room with workbenches all around the sides and a large table in the middle. Different tools are stored neatly in racks on the walls, and a gorgeous scent of wood and leather fills the air.

'Who works in here?' I immediately envisaged Santa's elves busy working away, but there's no one here.

'Grandad. It's his favourite place in the whole world,' Klaus says, looking around with a warm smile. 'He sometimes has a few friends over to help out, too, when we need stocking up.'

'It's magical.' I'd love to see his grandad making the wooden toys here. I'll bet it looks like a scene from a Christmas movie.

'It is,' Klaus looks quite dreamy as he nods, still looking around the room. Logs still line the walls in here, and there's no carpet on the wooden floor. Although I know there must be some hidden lighting somewhere, the whole room looks very rustic and traditional.

'I'm moving back home,' I blurt out.

Klaus turns to stare at me. 'Really?'

I nod. 'I've been offered a job at the jumper factory. In the advertising department. Well, doing some marketing as well, but mainly advertising. I start after Christmas, as soon as my notice is up over in Greenchurch.'

Klaus's handsome face lights up and he takes me in a big hug. 'That's fantastic news. I can't think of anything better.'

I giggle as he twirls me around. 'I'm not so sure Mum and Dad are so thrilled, to be honest, as it means moving back into my old room, but it'll only be until I find somewhere else to live.'

'I'm sure they'll love having you home, really,' he

assures me. 'I think you'll find they miss you just as much as you miss them.'

I hope he's right.

'When did all this happen?' he asks, his eyes bright with excitement.

'Yesterday. I didn't want to tell you over the phone.' I suddenly feel guilty for keeping it from him.

He shakes his head. 'No, it's not the sort of news you want to share like that,' he agrees. 'In person is much better. Especially as I get to do this.' He takes my lips in a lingering kiss that warms me right through and I close my eyes to savour every last second of it. It's the first time we've shared a 'proper' kiss, and, boy, I certainly hope it's not the last. This guy can *really* smooch.

When he finally releases my swollen lips I feel like I'm spinning, and I'm glad to still be in his arms, or I think I might fall over.

'I'm so proud of you,' he tells me, his voice soft and deep.

'Me?' *I think I was a toddler sitting on a potty the last time anyone said that to me.*

He nods. 'You've really turned everything around,' he says, smiling. 'Christmas, the German Market, Jumpers for Joy, your job... there's no limit to what you can do!'

'Hey, it wasn't all me,' I remind him, giggling. 'I

seem to remember you having a large hand in all of that.'

'I had nothing to do with your new job,' he points out. 'And I don't think I'd have been fired up enough to do so much if it hadn't been for you and your passion for this town.'

'You're the one who spoke to the town council. And I'm sure you had more to do with the whole town getting their decorations up than you're letting on,' I protest.

'I only decorated the hotel,' he insists. 'And spoke to that busybody at the clothes shop.'

I narrow my eyes at him, peering into his face. He looks innocent enough, but something tells me he's got a lot more influence around here than he's admitting.

'We make a great team,' I concede with a smile.

'Well now, no one's disputing that.' He kisses me once more, a lot gentler than earlier but no less enjoyable. He holds me in his arms for a while and I feel like I'm drifting on a cloud across a sunny sky. There's something about Klaus that just makes you feel good.

'I love spending time with you,' he murmurs, moving his head to look at me.

'I love it, too.' I fiddle with my bracelet, something that's become a bit of a habit recently.

'It's great to actually have some time to ourselves for a change,' he goes on, wistfully. 'We've both been so busy since we got here. Hopefully things'll calm down after the big day and we can actually enjoy each others' company.'

I nod. 'Except that I'll be going back to Greenchurch,' I remind him, as a horrid feeling of doom threatens to engulf me. 'Though it won't be for long. Just a couple of weeks, I think, if I can work the dates out right.' I refuse to let thoughts of that place bring me down, especially now.

He nods with a smile. 'That's true. Though there's nothing saying I can't come over and visit you while you're there, is there? I'm sure you could do with a hand packing up all your stuff ready to move back home.'

My heart lightens again. Klaus seems to have that effect on me.

'You're right. I'll have to get a van or something to move all my stuff. I'm sure I've got more now than when I moved in.'

'That's perfectly understandable,' he says, kindly. 'It's been a couple of years. You're bound to accumulate more belongings in that time, especially when it's your first place of your own.'

I smile, suddenly feeling vindicated for all the shopping sprees I've been on since I've been away from my mum's prying eyes. Not that she'd begrudge me anything, of course, but she *does* have an uncanny knack of reminding me about budgeting and bill-paying. *Sometimes I think she's too sensible for my own good!*

'Hey, you were going to tell me about this manager of yours.' I suddenly remember.

He grimaces. 'I was. It's nothing bad. It's just that he's clearly more interested in the modern games and equipment that we sell, and he spends more time in that part of the shop than the other.' He shakes his head. 'I can't blame him, because the layout of the shop doesn't help. Being segregated the way it is makes it almost like two shops in one, so it's hard for him to be in two places at once.'

'What about your part-timer?' I frown, remembering what Klaus told me before about being caught between his grandad and his dad. It would hardly be tactful to ask about joining the two parts together, although I can't help thinking that would be the ideal solution.

'Becky works mainly in the traditional side, but that's partly because there's only one till in each end.'

I nod. It makes sense.

'When we checked the books it was clear that the modern toys and games were making more than the traditional ones, which hurt Grandad quite a bit. He claims it's because Neal McLean, the manager, favours the other part of the shop and is encouraging shoppers to buy from there instead of the other toys.'

'Customers will buy what they want, and there's a huge difference between a young child's wooden toy and a teenager's game station or whatever,' I point out. 'Besides, surely you make more money on the higher-priced items?' As the words leave my mouth a great feeling of guilt overcomes me, and I wonder if it has something to do with the smell of wood that surrounds us.

'Is Grandad living in the past?' Klaus asks in not much more than a whisper. 'Is he clinging to the way things used to be while the rest of the world moves on? Are we wrong to keep selling old-fashioned wooden toys and games when most kids are growing up to prefer twenty-first century entertainment?'

I can see in his face that he's only voicing his concerns, but that he doesn't want to believe any of it.

'It is a business, after all,' he adds, thoughtfully, as sadness mars his gorgeous face.

I swallow hard. 'It *is* a business,' I agree, putting a hand on his arm. 'But it's a *family* business. Run by, and for *families*. Not just teenagers. I get that there's room for all the modern gadgets and gismos that kids grow to expect these days, but what about the youngsters? The toys your grandad makes are probably the safest on the market. He makes sure there are no loose bits, no jagged edges. Every single one is made individually with care and love—that's got to be better than all the mass-produced plastic rubbish out there on the market nowadays, surely?'

He nods, and I realise just how tense his face had become.

'Didn't you make any money yesterday with all the traditional toys?' I ask, gently.

'Yeah. A small fortune. Everyone loved what Grandad had made and they sold like hot cakes.' His eyes light up at the thought. 'He was so chuffed that they'd been so well-received.'

'There's room for both,' I tell him. 'They're just two completely different markets, that's all. You could think about running the shop as two separate businesses, or even physically turning it into two shops—maybe just put a door between them if it's easier. Or just leave them as they are, and have a manager for each side. One that's passionate about what they're selling. Either way, I think you owe it to your customers as well as your grandad to keep both avenues open.'

He beams at me, as a look of realisation and deter-mination crosses his face. 'You're right, Chris. I know exactly what I'm going to do.'

He takes me in his arms again and treats me to another leg-wobbling kiss. *I think I need to be right more often if that's the reward!*

15

'AND JUST WHAT KIND OF VIBE WERE YOU AIMING FOR, GRANDAD?'

We have to go back into the shop to ask Klaus's grandad for the key to the storage area where all the children's toys are kept ready for the big day. Apparently there's only one and his Grandad insists on keeping it on him at all times. Only a restricted few are allowed to go into the storage area, so I feel very privileged.

'Don't touch anything, will you?' the elderly man warns us, reaching into his pocket. 'It's all in strict order so I know what's what.' He gives a secretive smile as he hands over the key, which is much smaller than I imagined.

'That's so dainty,' I say to Klaus as we leave the shop. 'Is it for a padlock or something?' I was expecting a long key, like the type used for a mortice lock.

Klaus shrugs, stuffing it into his pocket. 'No, it's just a lock.'

We trudge around to the back of the building where I notice another large, log-cabin. My attention's drawn to a beautiful large house to one side of it, with a smaller house just nearby.

'Is this your home?' I ask, amazed at the gorgeous buildings.

He nods. 'Yep. That's my place over there.' He points. 'We can take a look around after, if you like?' There's still no electricity; it won't be connected up until after Christmas, but the rest of it's all ready. I've even had most of the furniture delivered so it should all be done by the time I move in.'

'You've already left your last place, haven't you?' I remember him talking about it in the taxi that night we met.

He nods. 'Yeah. All my stuff's in storage—not that there's much anyway. I was renting a furnished flat, so I didn't have to buy much while I was there. It was fun picking out stuff for this place, though.' He smiles, and I can guess he's desperate to move into his new home.

I decide not to mention that I'm also renting a small, furnished flat, which I've been in for less time than he was in his, but I've still got loads of belongings to move down with me. In fact, I think *I* might have to rent a storage unit, as it's certainly not going to all fit into my little bedroom at home.

'So, is your dad having the big house all to himself, then?' I frown. It's a beautiful family home, and I can't imagine Nick Saint rattling about in it all by himself.

'Sort of. Grandma and Grandad are planning to spend a lot more time down here, so they'll be staying there a lot of the time. It's also big enough for friends and family to stay in when they come to visit. Dad hasn't really bothered with the rest of the family much, preferring to keep himself to himself but Grandad insisted he have a house big enough to accommodate everyone, as they're always asking to visit, but Dad keeps putting them off.'

'That can't be all that nice for you?' I frown. 'Surely you want to see your family, too?'

He shrugs. 'I don't really know them,' he admits, leading me over to the storage building. 'But Dad agreed it would be nice to see them all again, so he approved the plans for the bigger house. It's been lovely to see how well he and Grandad have been getting along these past few days, actually. I think he's starting to come around to Grandad's way of thinking, at last.'

He puts the key into the tiny lock and opens the door.

The log cabin is decorated with thick, coloured tinsel that twinkles along with the fairy light that run right across the ceiling as well as along the edges. There's a huge Christmas tree in one corner with piles of presents underneath wrapped in an assortment of different coloured papers. The tree itself reaches to the ceiling and is a real feast for the eyes with numerous baubles, lights, decorations and candy canes hanging from it, hardly leaving an inch of it bare.

'Wow! It's just like Santa's grotto in here,' I manage, still taking it all in. 'And you've got a real tree,' I notice, with a smile. 'It smells gorgeous.'

Klaus nods, closing the door behind us. It's surprisingly warm inside, though I can't see any form of heating anywhere.

'Yeah, Grandad insists on a proper Christmas tree every year. It's still growing, of course, and we'll put it in the garden after New Year. If we'd managed to move in to the houses before Christmas we were going to take it through to Dad's place for the big day, but we'll have to wait another week yet.'

'It would have been nice to be in your new homes for Christmas,' I muse.

Klaus grins. 'If the house had been ready sooner, I might have come to Merryville earlier, and there's a chance I might not have met you,' he reminds me, putting an arm around my waist. 'Besides, this way we get to have Christmas dinner made for us at the hotel, instead of having to put up with Dad's burnt offerings.' He rolls his eyes. 'We usually try to do it between us, but he always takes over, so I generally leave him to it after the meat's in the oven.'

I giggle, before looking around the room again. There are stacks of presents in different wrapping, piled high along the left-hand wall.

'Your grandad's very well organised,' I remark.

'He has to be. We've only got tomorrow to finish getting everything ready. Then Christmas Eve is a very busy day for him. We've got the shop open in the morning and then he'll be taking all these to the party in the evening and handing them out to the children. That's why he's so strict about it all being in a certain order. It helps keep him on track.'

'It's amazing,' I tell him. 'And so's your grandad.'

Klaus smiles, holding me a little tighter. 'Come on, I'll show you my house.'

We go back outside and Klaus closes the door, then takes the key from his pocket. A sudden sound makes us both look around.

'I think someone's there,' Klaus says, frowning. 'Probably Grandad. I'll just check he's okay.' He hands me the key and goes over towards the workshop.

I quickly lock the cabin door with a shudder. The sky's a funny grey colour, and it looks like more snow is due to fall at any minute. There's an eerie silence surrounding me, which I hope is just because I'm on my own right now. Tucking the key into my pocket I look around a little. It still feels like someone's nearby, watching me, and I wonder if it might be an animal or something.

To my relief, Klaus comes back after a few minutes. 'It wasn't Grandad,' he says, shaking his head. He and Dad are still in the shop. It's quite busy in there, too.

'Maybe it was dog or something,' I suggest, reaching for his hand as he gets closer.

He nods. 'Could be. Or even one of the customers having a look around. They're not allowed this far back, but you always get one or two.'

'It's lovely and peaceful out here,' I muse, with a smile.

'Bit cold, though, eh? Come and see the house. Oh, and by the way, Grandad's going over to the hotel to work on his car, Comet, in a while, so he's offered for us to share the taxi.'

'Great.'

We go into the annexe, which is actually a three-bedroom house with its own little garden, complete with patio beneath all the snow, Klaus informs me. 'I'm hoping to have barbecues in the summer,' he goes on. 'I've got some all-weather outside seating coming after Christmas, too.'

'Are you a keen gardener?' I ask, as we step inside.

'Not really, though I quite like doing stuff like building planters and raised beds and stuff. Grandma and Grandad love planting things, though, so they've promised to help with all that.'

'You're very lucky,' I tell him with a smile. 'My grandparents died when I was really young. I don't remember them at all, just from photos that Mum's shown me.'

I wipe my feet on the doormat and Klaus wraps an arm around me. 'I'm sorry,' he says, softly. 'I didn't think. I'm always wittering on about the oldies and I never thought how you might feel.'

I look up at him with a smile. 'It's fine, honestly. I love yours, anyhow. And, to be honest, I probably talk about my mum without thinking how it might affect you.'

He raises his eyebrows. 'I've never really thought of it like that. Mums just seem to be what everyone has, so I'm well-used to people talking about theirs. It doesn't bother me at all.'

I nod, glad we're both on the same wavelength.

'Come on, we'll start with the kitchen,' he offers, leading me down the hallway.

'Oh, Klaus!' The kitchen is absolutely gorgeous; pale gold walls team beautifully with the oak units and table. Accessories are picked out in rich browns and dark ochre, giving a homely, warm vibe to the whole room.

His good taste follows through the house with a very pale green on the walls of the living room, with a cream-coloured suite and dark wooden cabinets. For the bedrooms he's chosen primrose yellow, pale blue and lilac, all with white furniture and plenty of silver accents.

'This is stunning,' I tell him with a smile, as we go back downstairs. 'You're so lucky to have all this.'

'I know,' he says, nodding. 'And I'll be living right next to my work, too, so I won't have to do much travelling.' He leans into me with a grin. 'At least Dad'll be happy. Grandad's been offering to lend me his car until I can get one of my own. I didn't need one when I was living in Higher Ludd as everything I needed was practically on my doorstep. The trouble is, Grandad's car much bigger and more powerful than anything I've ever driven,' he says, shaking his head. 'It would take some getting used to—I'd have to use 'P' plates until I really got the hang of it.'

I can't help giggling. 'I can just see you trying to come to grips with that huge hunk of metal.'

The words are barely out of my mouth when the front door opens and Klaus's grandad stamps his snowy feet on the mat. 'And just what's wrong with my car?' His eyes twinkle with mirth, setting me off giggling again.

'Nothing,' I assure him. 'I was just imagining Klaus trying to drive it, that's all.'

His grandad frowns at Klaus. 'Funnily enough, your dad seems to have the same problem with it.'

'I think I'd be better off driving a much less powerful car, Grandad,' Klaus says, tactfully.

'Besides, can you imagine what it would do for your street cred to have 'P' plates attached to your lovely car?' I giggle at the thought, and, thankfully, Klaus senior sees the funny side, too.

'I hadn't thought of that,' he admits. 'Hmm. Not quite the vibe I was going for, to be honest.'

'And just what kind of vibe *were* you aiming for, Grandad?' Klaus asks with a grin.

The old man opens his mouth, but must then realise he doesn't know what to say so he quickly closes it again.

'Is that the taxi outside?' I ask, hearing the rattle of a diesel engine.

'It is indeed. That's what I came to tell you,' Klaus senior replies. 'Did you want a lift back to the hotel? Your dad says he can handle the shop for this afternoon, so I can go and work on the car. I'm not rushing you if you want to stick around, but I just thought...'

'Yeah, it's probably about time we were heading back, actually,' Klaus says with a nod. He glances at his watch. 'Crikey, is that the time? No wonder I'm starving. Come on, we'll grab some lunch at the hotel.' He puts an arm around me and leads me back outside to where the taxi's waiting.

'THERE'S no one in the lounge, if you want to chill out this afternoon,' Margaret offers as she clears away our dishes after a delicious lunch of lamb shanks with roast potatoes, carrots and thick gravy. 'I'll bring your drinks through, if you like? Maybe a slice of chocolate cake?'

'Not for me, thanks, I'm off to work on the car,' Klaus's grandad says, wiping a napkin over his mouth. 'I want to look at that filter again.'

'What do you think?' Klaus turns to me with a smile. 'Fancy an afternoon lounging in front of the telly?'

'There are some good Christmas films on right now,' Margaret adds.

I groan. 'It sounds like my idea of heaven.'

Klaus and I go through and cuddle up on the sofa with a soft throw wrapped around us—not that it's particularly cold or anything; it just feels cosier that way.

'Here you go.' Margaret follows us in a few minutes later with a tray of tea and cake. 'Just holler if you want anything.'

I sit back, wallowing in the peace and comfort. 'This is the life.'

'What do you want to see?' Klaus asks, flicking on the TV. 'Love Actually's just started if you fancy it?'

I gape at him. '*Do* I? It's only the best film ever made,' I inform him exuberantly. 'But... are you sure it's what *you* want to watch?'

He grins. 'Guys can enjoy Christmas movies as

well, you know?' He puts down the remote control and snuggles against me.

'I get it.' I narrow my eyes at him, suspiciously. 'It's Kiera Knightly, isn't it? *That's* why you want to watch it. Admit it.' I tickle him, surprised and delighted at how much he squirms.

'I'm sure I don't know what you're talking about,' he protests, between squeals.

'Yes, you do.'

He shakes his head, still flinching from my prods and tickles. 'Why would I want her when I've got my own gorgeous girl sitting right next to me?'

I'm not sure what to say to that, and it stops me in my tickling tracks. I nod. 'Right answer.'

16

'...A BIT MORE GRATITUDE AND A
LOT LESS ATTITUDE'

Time always runs away with me this close to the big day, and this year is no exception. Dad needs me to help out in the factory for a few hours in the morning, so I rise early and get ready.

'The sooner you start, the sooner you can finish,' Dad says, chirpily when I join him at the breakfast table.

'It's still pitch black out there,' I grumble, looking out the window. 'Are you sure it's not still the middle of the night?'

'You'll be fine once you get started,' Mum assures me, putting a large teapot on the table before sitting opposite me. 'Your dad's hoping to close the factory tomorrow at lunchtime at the latest, so everything needs to be done before then.'

'We've got lots of deliveries to send out today,' Dad says, munching on his cereal. 'I just hope Dave Hesketh's on the ball.'

'He seemed quite organised when I was there the other day,' I say, buttering a slice of toast.

'Yeah, he's a capable guy,' Dad agrees. 'I just hope he can cope with all the pressure of today. Christmas is always a hard slog for logistics. Keith Polter's got his head screwed on the right way, though; I'm sure he'll be a great help.'

'That's the distributions manager, isn't it?' Mum asks, pouring out the tea. 'I like him.'

Dad nods. 'Bob's expecting to hear back from Jonathan Hudson again today, too,' he goes on. 'Apparently Stella's doing much better, and the whole family have been thrilled that we managed to pull the factory back from the brink, so to speak.'

I can't help the warm feeling that floods my stomach. It must have been awful being all the way over in Spain with a sick relative, knowing that the whole family business was about to collapse. They must have felt so helpless.

'Do you want some jam with that, love?' Dad passes over the dish, which he places next to my plate.

It's very unusual for me, but I find eating my toast quite an effort this morning. I can only assume it's because it's so early; my system hasn't woken up yet. Or it could be that my stomach's still full of butterflies after the romantic time I had with Klaus yesterday. I miss him already.

'Thanks, Dad.' It's really kind of him, but I can't really face it. 'Actually, I'm not that hungry yet. I think I'll pack up some food to take with me.'

'Good idea,' Mum says, as I finish my toast. 'You'll be starving later. Especially if you do end up working later than lunchtime.'

Dad nods. 'Yeah, the cafeteria won't be open today; the catering staff have all broken up for Christmas already. It's in their contracts, apparently.'

After another gulp of my tea, I push my chair back and steady my hands on the table as I get up.

'Ew!' My right hand slaps down right into the jam-dish.

Dad raises his eyebrows, looking quite bewildered, while Mum just shakes her head.

With a huff I go straight over to the sink and wash my hands, as the sticky raspberry pips get caught between my fingers. After that I open the cupboard to see what I can take for my snack.

'There's ham in the fridge if you want to make some sandwiches, love,' Mum offers. 'And some of that nice pickle you like.'

It's a great idea except that I really can't be bothered to make sandwiches right now. The thought of going to all that effort is exhausting enough.

'It's okay. I'll just grab some biscuits and stuff,' I

reply, noticing a packet of chocolate digestives on the shelf. There's also a box of iced mince pies that I'm sure no one will miss, along with a four-pack of chocolate bars. I scoop them all up into a carrier bag—a bag for life, of course—and then open the fridge for more inspiration. There's a big bottle of flavoured water that'll keep me going, as well as a couple of pork pies—which would also be great with that pickle, but I decide that's a bit messy to eat without a table, and I'm bound to be eating on the hoof.

I go into the hall to stuff the bag into my large handbag—no one wants to look like a bag lady—and pull on my boots.

Dad follows me through and starts putting on his coat.

I look up in surprise. 'Does Mum need a hand with the dishes?' I'd actually expected her to leave them until later so we could get straight to work, being as Dad seems so keen, but she's not even putting her outdoor shoes on yet.

'No, love. She said she'll do it.'

I frown as Mum strolls through to the doorway. 'Don't work too hard,' she says with a smile.

'What? Aren't you coming? I thought it was all shoulders to the wheel today? One final push, and all that.'

'It will be, but I'm sure you can manage without me,' Mum replies, shaking her head. 'The WI still need to get the baking done for tomorrow's party, and Joyce Roberts has gone down with the flu so we're all picking up the slack.'

'Poor Joyce. I hope she's okay,' Dad says, lacing his shoes.

'She's got her family staying for Christmas so they're all looking after her,' Mum replies with a nod. 'I thought I'd pop round this afternoon if I get a minute, just to see if there's anything they need.'

'Good idea.' Dad leans over and gives her a quick kiss before opening the front door.

My mind's still whirling with the idea that Mum's going to have time to pop in on Joyce today. I've got the whole morning working at the factory, and then I've promised to go over and help Klaus and his grandparents with all the presents for the children. He called me last night after I got home to say that Denise Blackenbury had got her numbers wrong, and they need even more toys than they'd catered for. I wish *I* could go and 'pop in' on people.

'You're looking very thoughtful, love.' Dad smiles as he unlocks the car and we both climb in.

'Yeah.' I pray he doesn't ask me what I'm thinking about—he really doesn't need to know.

As soon as we arrive at the factory, it's all systems go, as we're still producing some of the stock that needs to be delivered this afternoon, and haven't even started on tomorrow's yet. I go straight into the staff room to hang up my coat before pulling my overalls on over my jeans and Christmas jumper—today's delight is a cute teddy with a woolly hat, carrying a present, surrounded, of course, by snow.

Above the sounds of machinery, as soon as I go onto the factory floor, I can hear shouting. A group of people are over by the delivery exit having a huge argument. Obviously, I go straight over to investigate—not that I'm nosey or anything.

'These were supposed to go yesterday,' Molly, one of the senior supervisors is yelling. 'Why haven't they gone?'

Bethany and Emilee just shrug. 'We were told to stack them here ready to go,' Emilee points out. 'How were we to know they'd still be here this morning?'

'We need the space for those ones that will be starting to come off the production line in less than an hour.' Molly looks quite exasperated, and I'm sure it's the noise of the factory, and not the fact that she likes the sound of her own voice that's making her shout.

I can see the problem right away. That's why we're still producing stock today—we just don't have the room to store too much, which is why it usually goes straight onto the delivery lorries as soon as it's finished and labelled up.

'Who are these for?' I ask, squinting at one of the labels.

'Desired Designs over in Copperbridge,' Bethany replies. 'They should have been delivered last night.'

'Shall I go and have a word with Keith Polter, see what the holdup is?' I ask Molly.

She sighs. 'Would you? I've got to get today's batch ready or we'll fall behind and no one wants to have to work late tonight.'

I nod with a smile and have to go the long way around to the distribution department, being as the doorway's already full of heavy boxes.

Dad's throwing his hands up in the air when I arrive, and Bob Robinson's shaking his head. Keith Polter looks like he's just aged ten years in the two days since I last saw him, and my stomach churns with dread.

'Molly needs to know what the problem is,' I say, a little sheepishly. *To be honest, I'm not so sure I really want to know now, after all.*

'One of the lorries was on its way back from Southbridge last night when it had a problem with the brakes,' Dad explains, looking worried sick.

I put my hands to my mouth. 'Oh, no.'

'It's okay, love.' He puts a reassuring hand on my arm. 'It was one of our best drivers and he knew just what to do. He managed to slow down through the gears and pull over. He's fine. We've got a recovery vehicle out there now taking a look at it.'

Well, that certainly explains why the delivery

hadn't been taken last night. The sight of a policeman coming into the room alerts me there's more to it than that, though.

'Mr. Robinson?' the guy asks, coming over to us.

'That's me.' Bob turns to speak to him.

'I've got some officers examining the damage now, sir. It looks like you've got your work cut out for you, so I won't keep you any longer than need be. I just need a statement from you, if that's all right, sir?'

'Of course. Come up to my office.' The two men leave the room and I turn back to Dad with my eyebrows raised in question.

'This isn't general knowledge yet.' Dad lowers his voice. 'But it seems that there's been some sabotage to our lorries. Every one of them had its tyres slashed last night. Nothing's moving until the police have finished their investigation, and we've got hold of some replacements. Needless to say, none of the tyre companies are open yet, and some won't even be opening today at all, having already closed for Christmas.' He runs a hand across his face. 'We'll be lucky to get everything delivered on time at this rate.'

'Oh, Dad.' I know I'm at work, but I can't help throwing my arms around him. He looks so helpless, all of a sudden. 'Do we know who did it?'

He sighs. 'No, love. They managed to smash the CCTV cameras so we couldn't get any footage. They also took advantage of a couple of security lights that had blown a couple of days ago—clearly not the accident we'd assumed it to be—so the security guards didn't even clock them. They certainly knew what they were doing.'

'But, how did they get in? The gates are always locked until one of the security guys opens them when a delivery goes in or out.

'They came in on foot, so they only needed to access the little side gate,' Dad says. 'The only people who have the key to it are management, and, even then, only those who work down here. No one else would ever need one.'

'And they're all accounted for?' I ask.

A loud snort reminds me that Keith Polter's still standing there. I stare at him.

'Yes, there are none missing,' Dad says.

I narrow my eyes at Keith, who's obviously got something to say.

'So, are they thinking it's an inside job?' I frown at both men. It's hard to believe that anyone who's gone through all this recent upheaval with the company would do anything like this. We were all pulling together—weren't we?

'It's probably best not to speculate, love,' Dad urges. 'It's in the hands of the police now.'

I narrow my eyes at him, certain he knows more than he's telling me.

'So, if it's not an inside job, it's certainly someone

on the outside who knows about that side gate and has —or *had*—access to it.'

Keith smiles and I know I've hit the nail on the head.

I shake my head. 'It wouldn't have taken much for Drew Chapman to have had another key cut while he was here,' I say. 'And who would have a better motive than the guy who's about to go down for fraud and theft? Have the cops picked him up yet?'

'This stays between us,' Dad replies, sharply. 'Nothing's been proven yet, okay?'

I nod. 'Of course. What are we telling the staff? Someone sabotaged our delivery trucks but we don't know who? You don't think they'll all put two and two together like I just did, then?'

'For now we're not mentioning the sabotage. Just a problem with a couple of the lorries,' Keith replies.

'Okay. But we've got a logistics problem if we're going to continue producing the orders we need for today. The load that was supposed to go last night's still waiting in our doorway. Is there any way we can get it moved to make room for the next batch in less than an hour?' I bite my lip, knowing it's probably the last thing Dad needs to worry about right now.

'I'll ask Dave Hesketh to get some of his guys onto it,' Dad promises. 'Just be careful what you say, though, okay, Chris?'

He gives me one of those looks he used to give me when I was little. A sort of *warning* look.

'Of course, Dad. You know you can always count on me.' As I'm walking away I'm sure I can hear someone snort again.

For the next couple of hours we're all rushed off our feet as we try to get the next batch of jumpers produced and boxed up ready for a delivery that might never happen—not that anyone knows that, of course. Well, not in my department, anyway.

I take my ten minute break and head towards the staff room to grab something to eat, absolutely ravenous by now. I pull out a pork pie from my bag and fish about for my phone.

'Oh no.' There are several missed calls from Klaus, as well as a couple of text messages: *Have you got the key to the store room?* And *Call me as soon as you can—it's urgent.*

I'm more disturbed at the lack of kisses at the ends of his messages, than the fact that he's misplaced a darn key. Why on earth would *I* have a key to his store room? I remember distinctly his grandad handing it to him. Surely it's not my fault if he's—oh no!

Quickly I delve into my coat pockets but it's not there. What I do find, however, is a hole. Just a little one in the corner of my right-hand pocket. Not big enough for much to escape down it and into the lining —but maybe a small key...

Chomping on the pork pie, I furtle about, feeling around the lining for the little, hard object. It takes a couple of tries, but eventually I find it, wedged between the lining and the thick hem of the coat. *Damn!*

I quickly call Klaus who answers right away.

'Chris! We need that key. Have you got it?' He sounds quite frazzled.

'Yes. I'm sorry, Klaus. It was in my pocket. In the lining, actually. You see, there was a hole and—'

'Can you bring it over? Grandad hit the roof with me when he realised I hadn't returned it to him yesterday. I'd completely forgotten at first that you had it.' I've never heard that edge to his voice before and it's clear that he's worried sick. I feel awful that he got into trouble with his grandad over it, too. I can't imagine the old guy losing his temper, but I suppose everyone's human.

'Of course. I'm really sorry. I'll get it over to you as soon as I can.'

'Thanks. We're absolutely manic over here or I'd come and fetch it. But Grandad needs to get into the store room to do a final count of the gifts, and he can't let the children down on Christmas Eve.'

'Yep. Okay. I'll just have to speak to Dad and get permission to leave and then I'll hop in a taxi,' I promise.

'Thanks, Chris. I really appreciate it.'

And I'd appreciate a bit more gratitude and a lot less

attitude, I want to tell him, but instead I just hang up. Did we just have our first row? Or was that when we were discussing iced mince pies the other day? My stomach roils. I thought we were getting on so well—especially after the lovely day we had yesterday—but maybe we just keep arguing without me even noticing...

17

'OKAY, SO THIS IS THE POINT WHERE SHE'S JUST ABOUT LOSING MY SYMPATHY'

I can't help feeling a bit disappointed, if I'm honest. Stuffing the phone back into my bag, and another pork pie into my mouth, I quickly close my locker.

'Aren't you supposed to be working?' Melanie suddenly appears in the doorway with a supercilious expression. 'I just heard Molly yelling your name. Just because your dad's a manager doesn't mean you can just skive off, you know?'

Oh no!

'I'm just going,' I tell her, accidentally spitting out bits of pastry from the pie I'm hurriedly trying to finish.

'Oh, that's so gross!' Melanie jumps back out of the way.

She's lucky. I was hoping to go to the loo before I

returned to my shift, too.

'I'm really sorry about that.' Okay, so this time it might not be so much of an accident as another shower of Melton Mowbray's finest heads in her direction, but she'd think me rude if I didn't apologise, wouldn't she? And I couldn't have that!

I rush through to the factory floor only to find the place buzzing with people huddling together in little groups talking excitedly.

'There you are, Chris.' Molly comes straight over to me. 'You'll never guess what's happened.'

I might, actually.

'According to Jim Whitley in distributions, someone's sabotaged all the delivery lorries!' Her eyes are wide as she tells me and I know I should mimic her for effect, but I just can't. She quickly narrows her eyes at me. 'You *knew*, didn't you?'

'It's supposed to be kept quiet until an official announcement's made,' I tell her. 'What has the management team told you?'

She straightens her back, her lips tightening. 'Well, clearly not as much as they've told *you!*'

'It wasn't like that,' I plead with her. 'Honestly, Molly, I wanted to tell you but I was sworn to secrecy until the police finished their investigation.'

'So, it's okay for *you*—who doesn't even work here officially—to know all about it, whereas a *senior supervisor*, ergo *me* doesn't get told anything?' Her pretty face

turns red as she stares at me, and I can kind of understand her point.

I shake my head. 'You're right, Molly. You should
have been told. In fact, I was under the impression that
you were going to be. I suppose they must have just
been so busy over there with the police and making
statements and stuff that no one got as far as informing
you yet. I'm really sorry that happened. It's not right.' I
hope I sound as sincere as I feel.

'No, it's not.' She looks more hurt than annoyed
now, and I'm not actually sure which is worse. She
gives a big sigh. 'Do they have any suspicions about
who it might have been?'

I stare at her, not sure what to say to that. It's not
often I'm at a loss for words, so this is all very peculiar
to me—not to mention horrid.

'I didn't get to speak to the police,' I tell her. 'It was
only Bob Robinson that I saw actually talking with one
of them.'

'Well *he's* not going to tell me anything, is he?' She
sounds quite derisory, and I'm not sure where my
loyalties lie right now. I mean, I can clearly see it from
both sides.

One thing I *do* know, however, is that Dad'll kill me
if I blab.

She huffs again. 'Well, anyway. We've been told to
keep producing these orders, regardless of whether or
not they get delivered today. Which actually sounds

like a right waste of time, if you ask me, but then, no one *is* asking me, are they? Neither are they telling me anything because, of course, I don't count, do I?'

Okay, so this is the point where she's just about losing my sympathy.

She straightens herself up again, as though suddenly taking stock of her position. 'Right, I need you to go down and help get that last order packed and labelled. Someone from logistics is going to come and tell us where to put it while we wait to see what's happening with the lorries, so, for now, you'll need to just stack them as best you can. We're already running behind.' She rolls her eyes.

'Actually, Molly, I was going to ask if…?'

I can see by her expression that the answer will be no, so I stop abruptly. In fact, I've got the distinct impression she might say a lot more than just 'no', and in a very loud voice if I ask what I was going to ask so I decide not to. Maybe I'll be able to sneak out in a while without her noticing, or something?

I go back to the packaging department, only to find the atmosphere not much better there.

'How's it going?' I try to sound chirpy, in the hope it might lighten the tension a little. It doesn't.

'Oh, so you're actually going to do some work today, are you?' Melanie appears from the centre of a group of girls—her favourite place to be, I imagine—and sneers at me.

Damn! I've got little chance of disappearing from here without being noticed with her around. I don't know why she's taken a dislike to me, but haven't got time to worry about that now.

'Molly just asked me to come down—she said you guys needed some help.' I smile sweetly, not being derisory at all.

Melanie just scowls at me, but one of the others pipes up, 'There just isn't the space to put anything.'

'Yeah, and I think we've got these orders jumbled up,' Bethany announces with a grimace. 'A couple of men from logistics came over to help, but they've piled some of the boxes up before we could put the labels on.'

I roll my eyes. 'Very helpful.'

'So, come on, genius, how are you going to solve all this, then?' Melanie's scathing remarks hold no bounds.

'Well, we'll have more boxes coming off the machines shortly, so we need to make some room for them. Why don't some of you stack up all the labelled boxes onto those pallets, and we'll have to open the unlabelled ones over here and get them marked up?'

As predicted, Melanie and her gang all go to do the opposite job to me, for which I'm eternally grateful. I have to get a couple of logistics guys back with forklift trucks to move the stock around—those boxes are heavy!—but they don't seem to mind.

'Any news about the lorries?' I ask one of them, who I think is called Matt.

'They've managed to source some new tyres, so we can get some of the trucks running as soon as they're fitted, but we can't get hold of enough for the rest.

'Will we still get the orders out in time?'

He shrugs. 'I dunno. Obviously we're going to prioritise what's needed first, but whether we get them all delivered today is anybody's guess—especially as we're a driver down. And we'll have even more to get out in the morning, so we're going to be hard-pressed.'

My eyes widen. 'Was that guy hurt last night? The one with the brake problem?'

Matt shakes his head, making his light-ginger curls fall into his face. He's really quite handsome. 'He was a bit shaken up, and had to walk miles before he could get a signal to let anyone know what had happened and arrange a lift home.' He lowers his voice. 'The police are investigating whether the brakes were actually an accident or not, in the light of what's happened here, so the poor guy's been down the station for the past couple of hours.'

My stomach churns at the thought. 'He could've been killed. If it wasn't an accident, someone will be facing charges for attempted murder.' My face heats up at the horror of it all. It really doesn't bear thinking about.

'We'll have to wait and see what the cops come up

with,' Matt says, his concerned expression telling me I'm right.

'We're running out of room over here!' Melanie shouts over, clearly irritated. I secretly wonder if she fancies Matt.

'How long before we can get some of these onto the first lorry?' I ask him.

He pulls a radio from his pocket and asks the question of someone in the distribution section.

'They've just got the first one ready and are bringing it round to the loading bay now,' he tells me with a smile.

'Great, the first order that needed to go is already in position ready to go through,' I tell him, feeling more than a little relieved. 'We need to sort these out to see what's what, and then they can go down after that.'

He nods. 'Right, I'll get a couple more of our guys up to help.'

As Matt leaves me, his hair looks golden under the fluorescent lights, resembling a halo, and I can't help thinking how appropriate that is.

It's another hour before I manage to sneak off to the loo. Of course, I go via the staff room and grab my phone. There are even more messages from Klaus waiting for me, and I dread opening them, but, once safely ensconced in one of the cubicles of the ladies' toilets I take a deep breath and face the music.

'Where are you, Chris? How much longer will you be?'

That was sent less than an hour after I spoke to him, so he was obviously expecting me to leave straight away. I would have, too, if it hadn't been for Molly. And Melanie. Oh gosh, this is all going horribly wrong.

The next message sounds a little more concerned, which I find heartening.

Chris, are you okay? By our reckoning you should have been here ages ago. Has something happened? Call me, I'm worried.

The feeling clearly didn't last long, as the next message is back to: *How much longer will you be? Grandad's going frantic not being able to get into the store room. We need to get the children's gifts ready in time.'*

I can't help feeling a bit irked at his attitude, to be honest. I mean, how stupid is it to only have one key in the first place? Surely they should be covered for any eventuality, especially with something as important as that? And I get that they're rushed off their feet and can't come and fetch it, but don't they think *my* job's important, too? We went to a lot of effort to save this factory; what would be the point if it lets everyone down at the most crucial time?

I quickly message him back. *Sorry. Massive problems here today. I'll explain later. Haven't left yet, but will as soon as I can. Was supposed to finish at lunchtime but looks doubtful.* I check the time and shake my head. It's already half past eleven. Then I add: *Not allowed to take phone on factory floor, btw.*

He already knows I can't have my phone with me all the time when I'm working. As it is, I've had to slide the lovely bracelet he bought me right up my forearm so no one sees it. Dad would go mad if he knew, but I just don't want to take it off. Besides, it's not as if I control the machinery or anything, is it? They've got skilled people for that.

It's actually a couple more hours before Dad comes through to say I can go home. He looks a lot more relaxed than earlier, thank goodness.

'Thanks for your help, love.'

'That's okay, Dad. I've got to get to Klaus's shop but I'll see you at home later.'

'Hopefully there won't be too much to do tomorrow, so you'll get some time to yourselves in the afternoon.' Dad smiles and I just grin.

According to Klaus, Christmas Eve is their busiest day of the year, so I doubt he'll have much time to spend with me, even if I do finish early here. Of course, I'll offer to help him, but something tells me the Saint family run like a well-oiled machine when they're busy. I only have to think back to the German Market, and how they all worked together then.

I pull my coat on, feeling in the hemline for the key. I'll have to unpick a part of the hem to retrieve it when I get there; the last thing I want to do is lose it now.

After a chorus of goodbyes and thank yous, I head outside, pulling my phone from my pocket. The snow's really thick, where it's been falling all day, and there are only a few cars on the road.

I ring the taxi firm only be told they're inundated with calls right now, and advising me to call back later. *Typical!*

There's nothing else for it, but to start walking. I quickly text Klaus to let him know the situation, and that I'm on my way.

'Great. We really need that key.'

His reply cuts me like a knife. It doesn't sound as though he's in the least bit bothered that I'm going to have to walk for miles to get to him, or that I've already had a harrowing morning at work—all he cares about is that damn key!

I stomp through the snow, trying to remind myself that it's Christmas and I should be happy. Everything got sorted at the factory, and it looks like all the deliveries will be made on time, after all. Organisation is well under way for the Merryville Christmas Party and it sounds like we're expecting a good turnout, as usual —it's the most magical night of the year.

'Jingle bells, jingle bells,' I sing along to myself, my feet hitting the snow in time to the music in my head, and I soon feel much happier.

I'm walking down a quiet country road, singing at the top of my voice now—well, there's no one around, and Noddy Holder never sings quietly, does he?— admiring the typical Christmas card-look of the surrounding countryside. There's a thick pile of snow on top of the hedges on either side of me, but I can still see over them to the fields and farms in the distance. Robins are hopping about on the road in front of me and I can't help smiling at them.

I suddenly feel a shudder through my body. I stop singing and notice how quiet it is around me. Deathly quiet. That horrid feeling that I'm being watched cloaks me in fear again, and I sense the aura of impending doom.

'Don't be silly,' I tell myself aloud.

The road is very narrow and winding, and I'm aware that the dense snow would swallow the sound of footsteps. I roll my eyes at myself. No one would be walking down here today. *I'm* only here because I have no choice. It's nearly Christmas Eve. Sensible people will be at home in front of a roaring fire drinking eggnog by now. I wish *I* was sensible.

It's probably the silence that's got me feeling so jittery, I decide, taking a deep breath. I never did like quietness. I pull the hood of my duffle coat over my head and tighten the scarf around my neck, as the cold seeps in. My bag is safely across my body, allowing my arms to be free to swing as I walk, and my gloves are really cosy. There's only a couple more miles to go, and someone's bound to drive down here sooner or later and offer me a lift. *I've got this!*

With a confident smile, I burst into my best impression of Mariah Carey, even doing a little dance as I trudge down the road. I have a theory that if you think positively, positive things happen to you, so I'm thrilled when a car horn toots in harmony to my singing—*well, in my head, anyway!*

I hop onto the snow-covered grass verge and turn with a smile as a black car pulls up beside me.

'Fancy a lift, love?'

Now, normally I wouldn't dream of accepting a ride from a stranger but this is Merryville where everyone looks out for each other. It sounds corny, I know, but this is probably the safest place on earth. *Usually.*

18

'...WHEN HE OPENS HIS MOUTH I NOTICE HIS TEETH ARE EVEN WONKIER THAN HIS HAIRCUT'

My smile fades as I recognise the man who's getting out of the passenger-side right next to me.

'No, thanks.' I try to keep walking, but the guy clearly has other plans.

'Get in here!'

Running in thick snow isn't as easy as it looks in the films—or in Mariah Carey videos—and I find myself having to haul my boots out of every step. I can hear him thudding along behind me, his breath panting hard. Then his arm grabs mine, swinging me around. I fall into the snow, but he's still got a tight grip on me and drags me to my feet again.

'Come on.' His voice is gruff as he yanks my arm painfully.

'No,' I yell in the vain hope that someone will hear

and come running to my rescue. No such luck. *Okay, so I knew it was a long shot, having not seen a soul for the past couple of miles, but it had to be worth a try.*

'I am not going anywhere with you, Drew Chapman!' I tell him as he throws me into the back seat of the car and climbs in after me.

'Oh, yes you are!'

There's a click as the doors are locked by the driver, and we tear off through the snow without a thought for any vehicle that might be coming in the opposite direction on the one-track country lane.

'You think you're so clever, don't you?' Drew snarls at me, still gripping me tightly.

'You're hurting me.'

'That's right.' He gives a smug sneer.

'What do you want?'

'Wouldn't *you* like to know?' He looks quite menacing, which causes my stomach to jolt even worse than his friend's erratic driving does.

'That *is* why I asked, Einstein.' I give him an incredulous look in return.

He narrows his eyes at me. 'You came into our factory and caused me a lot of trouble, young lady.'

I raise my eyebrows. 'Why? Couldn't you get the barf stains out of your shoes?' I notice he's wearing black boots today – maybe leather or polyurethane: either way, something washable.

'Those shoes cost a lot of money and you ruined them!'

I narrow my eyes at him. 'So, that's what this is all about? A pair of smelly shoes?'

'They weren't smelly until you vomited all over them!'

'That's a matter of opinion,' I reply, raising my eyebrows. I find that a bit of bravado works wonders for the nerves, but my mind's reeling about what exactly is going on here.

The driver laughs, much to Drew's annoyance.

'Oh, shut up!' I'm not sure if that's aimed at me or the driver, to be honest, but I'm not deterred by it.

'You weren't known as 'old smelly feet' for nothing, you know.' No one actually called him that, but it can't help to shatter his confidence a little.

He balks, and I think it's actually working.

The driver seems to find it hysterical.

'Why would anyone call me that? That's rubbish and you know it.' Drew tuts, but I can see by the tenseness of his jaw that it's got him rattled.

'Why do you think, Sherlock? It certainly wasn't because of your bad breath.' His eyes widen and his whole body stiffens next to mine. 'Just shut up.' *Okay, so that one was definitely aimed at me.*

The driver's shoulders shake as he laughs even louder, and I can imagine Drew having words with him later.

'I thought you were telling me what exactly I've done to deserve all this,' I protest. Not that I can't guess, mind you. It seems he *did* recognise me that day at Jupiter Jumpers, after all.

'You stole from us,' he snaps.

'*You* stole from Jumpers for Joy,' I point out.

'I did not. They *owed* me.'

'You know full well you took their designs and their labels and tried to pass off your second-rate rubbish as their stock. Well, people know quality when they see it, and they certainly didn't find any in *your* products.' I feel a little unnerved that he's getting so angry.

He shakes his head, clearly seething. 'You'll pay for this!'

I don't like the sound of that, nor the expression on his face, so I say nothing and just stare out the window. I don't really want to know what he's got in store for me, because I'm planning to get away just as soon as I can. The adrenalin rush I got when he first grabbed me seems to have worn off and I'm starting to shiver, partly from cold and partly from nerves.

Judging by the scenery it looks like we're heading for Showford. *Deep joy!* I recognise the road and the grey buildings in the distance. There are some lovely houses in this town—and even lovelier people—but the large built-up expanses spoil it for me, somehow. Although, their local council are obviously really good at planting trees and keeping some green areas, as parts of it are absolutely stunning.

A familiar ringing sound from my bag makes Drew pounce. 'Give me that bag!'

'It's only got my lunch in it,' I protest as he pulls the strap over my head, catching some of my hair painfully in the process.

It's no good. He quickly fishes out my phone and switches it off, but not before sneering at the screen.

'Klaus, eh? I suppose that's the little moron who was pretending to own a business that needed stocking up, then? Didn't have the sense to think we'd look him up, did he?' He shakes his head, derisively.

I bite my tongue. It's such a shame he had to ring— and a shame I hadn't put my phone on silent, though I didn't have any cause to. I had hoped that I could call for help as soon as Drew left me alone, but that was clearly too much to ask. Now I've even lost my lunch as well, and I've suddenly realised I'm famished.

'I'm supposed to be helping with preparations for the Christmas party this afternoon,' I point out. 'People will notice if I'm not there.'

Drew snorts loudly. 'I doubt that.'

'But I'm expected to be there. People are relying on me.' I feel slightly panicked at the thought. I don't want anyone to think I've let them down, but what can I do?

'Don't worry. I'll take care of your phone. I'll let everyone know the reason why you're not there;

because you couldn't be bothered.' He gives a cruel laugh and I can't help thinking how good he'd be in a pantomime. He'd make Abanazar look like a saint!

We turn in towards the trading estate and my heart sinks as Jupiter Jumpers looms before us. The whole area is deserted as everyone's obviously closed down for Christmas. My nerves get the better of me as I study 'old smelly feet' beside me, wondering if he really is a killer. I certainly hope not, and it seems a bit extreme for just throwing up on his shoes—okay, so I may have had something to do with the closure of his business, too—but he *is* a desperate man, possibly facing a prison sentence. He might feel that he's got nothing to lose.

'Notice anything about this place?' Drew chides as he pulls me from the car. 'Anything about how quiet it is around here?' His jaw stiffens as he looks at me.

'It *is* very quiet.' I agree with him as I'm sure that's what he wants.

The driver emerges from the vehicle, clapping. 'Ooh, she's very bright this one, isn't she?'

It's the first time I get to see more than just the bald patch on the back of his head, and I have to admit I'm a bit disappointed. He's got to be in his fifties, with a scruffy moustache and pockmarks on his face. He's very tanned, and when he opens his mouth I notice his teeth are even wonkier than his haircut.

'Not as bright as she'd like to think.' Drew snarls as

he pushes me towards the entrance to the building, where a couple of men are waiting.

'Oh, this is the one, is it?' I don't recognise the portly guy in the suit, but I imagine he's probably the general manager or something, judging by his manner.

'Yep. Caused us all that trouble—as well as ruining my Gucci's.' *Drew's really not going to let that go, is he?*

The other man laughs. 'Ha! At least she's got taste. Those things were awful, mate!'

There's a slam as the driver shuts the door behind us, and I hear the grating sound of a bolt being slid across. I shudder, as this seems to be becoming more real by the minute.

'Does anyone know she's missing yet?' The boss asks, as we all walk past reception and down a corridor.

'Na. The boyfriend rang earlier but I cut him off,' Drew tells him.

The boss stops and turns to him. 'Cut him off? Why the hell did you do that? You should've just let it ring and left it unanswered.'

Drew frowns, his grip on my arm tightening painfully. 'What difference does it make? I didn't speak to him.'

'I told you, we don't want to arouse suspicion.'
Good luck with that! I roll my eyes.

'She's expected somewhere. Supposed to be

helping out with a party or something,' the driver offers as we all start walking again.

'Sorry, Cinderella, you won't be going to the ball this time,' the boss says, with a sneer.

I narrow my eyes at him but say nothing. It's usually safer that way, and right now I feel like I'm really in a lot of danger. I wonder how many more of their gang are here.

We go into a large office where I'm unceremoniously dumped on a chair in front of the desk while the boss takes pole position. Drew finally releases my arm but stands right next to me while the other two just stand around, watching.

'Right, Christina Moss,' the boss says, clasping his hands in front of him on the table. 'You've got a lot of explaining to do.'

My heart's racing as I look at his round, red face, trying to ignore the grey hairs sprouting from his nose.

'What do you want to know?' I swallow hard, aware that my voice isn't quite as loud as I'd intended.

'Well, perhaps you could explain the sudden demise of this place, after your visit the other day?' He waves a hand to indicate the factory. 'Or why the whole of my management team are undergoing legal proceedings at the county court? Or even why several of us were called into the police station this morning to answer a lot of *very* awkward questions?' His jaw gets tenser as he speaks and the atmosphere in the room is almost claustrophobic.

I shrug, not really wanting to get into an argument about this. He knows the answers already so there's nothing I can add that's going to help the situation.

'Are you going to answer me?' His shout makes me wince.

'I don't know what you want me to say,' I admit in a small voice.

He narrows his eyes at me. 'Your father is Noel Moss, isn't he?'

I'm suddenly concerned for my old man's safety. What are they planning to do to him?

'It's all right; you don't need to answer that one.' He shakes his head. 'We know exactly who you are. That's why you're here.'

'What do you want with me?' I can't keep the tremble from my voice, more's the pity. I was hoping to brazen this out, but I'm feeling more and more vulnerable as time goes on.

'Revenge,' the boss replies, flippantly. 'You took something of ours—this place—and now we're taking something of yours; your freedom. And something of your Dad's, of course. We all know he's Bob Robinson's right-hand man, even if he hasn't got the title yet, and we also know how much fuss he'll cause when he realises you've been taken.'

'Kidnapped.' I clarify in not much above a whisper.

He gives a supercilious grin. 'Yes.'

'But what's this got to do with my dad? Surely Bob Robinson's the man you should be worried about? He's the general manager.' I take deep breaths to calm myself down, as panic rises inside me.

The guy shakes his head. 'Bob Robinson wouldn't have thought of all this,' he assures me. 'He's not clever enough, everyone knows that. But your dad's a different matter. He's bright. *Too* bright. He put you up to all this, didn't he? Admit it, it was all *his* idea.'

'No. He didn't know half of what we were doing—and certainly had no idea Klaus and I were coming here. That's all on me.' *Okay, so I know it wasn't all my idea, but I don't want him roping everyone else into this nightmare.*

He shakes his head. 'I doubt that.'

I'm not sure I like the insinuation that I'm not clever enough to have done all this, but I can see how aggravated he's looking, so I let it go.

He notices the driver having a whispered giggle with the other man and frowns at them angrily. I'm sure I heard the words 'old smelly feet' being uttered, but, again, I say nothing.

There's a pinging sound and the boss checks his watch. He jumps to his feet. 'Right, we've got three minutes. You two take her down.' He points to Drew and the driver. He nods to the other guy. 'We'll go wait for the chopper.'

My legs turn to jelly as Drew hauls me from my chair.

'Be careful with her, old smelly feet,' the other man says with a chuckle. 'You don't want to hurt her.' He mutters something to the boss and they both burst out laughing, while Drew tightens his grip on my arm.

'That's what *you* think,' Drew mutters under his breath.

As I'm yanked out the door and over to the lift I can hear the sound of a helicopter getting nearer.

'Have you got the key?' The driver's asking Drew, but it immediately reminds me of the key in the lining of my coat. The key Klaus and his grandad are desperate for! I feel sick thinking how much I've let them down.

'Of course.' Drew's lips are tight as he replies.

We seem to go down a really long way in the lift before it stops and I'm pushed out and into a little store-room nearby. It smells damp and musty, and I suppose it hasn't been used in a while.

'You stay there,' Drew says, shoving me inside. 'And don't bother shouting; there'll be no one to hear you. The whole place is empty and no one's likely to return to the estate until after Christmas, so I should save your breath.'

'But I could die in here!' I wail, suddenly wanting to cry.

'Good job you brought your lunch, then; at least it won't be from starvation—well, not for while, anyway.' He throws my bag at me before both men leave the room, locking the heavy door after them.

19

'HONESTLY, NODDY HOLDER'S GOT
A LOT TO ANSWER FOR!'

I feel better after a chocolate bar and a good cry.

It's quite dark in here, and I notice there's no light switch. The room is just a square box with nothing in it—except me—and not even a window. There's a sort of vent-thing high up with metal bars across it, that looked like it had glass over it at one time, judging by the jagged edges around it, but all it's doing now is letting the snow in, so it wouldn't be a usable room even if the factory was still running. Despite the draught, I'm happy knowing that at least I won't suffocate in here. I can't rule out hypothermia, though!

I've already pulled everything out of my bag in the vain hope that 'old smelly feet' might have just dropped my phone back in here, but he didn't. I like the idea of all his colleagues calling him that from now on, too—providing they get to see each other once they're caught and behind bars, that is.

I take a swig of water from the large bottle I brought with me, and glance at my watch. It's nearly half past five. It's been hours since I left the factory; surely someone's noticed I've gone missing by now?

Klaus rang earlier, so he's obviously concerned—at least about the key, if not me. I feel a bit miserable thinking about how he was in his texts earlier. I wonder if I've just read them all wrong—that's the problem with messages as opposed to face to face conversations, I suppose. He was so lovely yesterday, and we spent such a wonderful afternoon curled up together on Margaret's sofa watching films. It felt quite romantic being so close to him, even when we didn't speak to each other. I could really get used to that. *Some of my best friendships are when we don't speak to each other—I can't think why!*

Thinking of Klaus, I reach for my bracelet but it's not where I expected. I tense as I run my right hand further up my left arm, but there's no sign of it. It must have broken and fallen off when I fell, or when Drew yanked me back up out of the snow!

Tears prick the outer edges of my eyes as I realise it's lost, probably buried under six feet of snow by now, or run over by a car on that back road. I loved wearing it as it reminded me of that lovely time we had at the German Market. I told Klaus I never wanted to take it off. Now he'll think I didn't mean it, or that he doesn't mean that much to me. But he does, I realise. More than he can know. I miss him, and wish so much that he was here now. I sniff loudly, and it almost echoes in the growing darkness.

It's so quiet here, and I've never felt so alone. Knowing that no one is likely to come to the trading estate until after Christmas is bad enough, but no one is going to come to the factory for ages, now that Jupiter Jumpers has closed down. Why would they? I'd imagine their lease will run for a while yet, stopping anyone else from taking the place over, and if those four have fled the country in a helicopter, you can bet no one else will come here.

The good thing is that Dad knew where I was headed, and I'd already told Klaus I was on my way, so they'll know by now that I'm actually missing. Will they be out looking for me already? Would they think to come all the way out here? I can only hope. And eat biscuits. It's the only things that'll keep me going now.

I MUST HAVE FALLEN ASLEEP, because I wake up to find it getting light outside. There's only a slither of sunlight creeping through the grated window, but it's enough to see my watch, which tells me it's half past six. I've survived the whole night out here on my own. Okay, so

I slept through it, but that's probably because I was so exhausted after working so hard at the factory, followed by all that walking. I must have trudged along for miles in that snow.

With a shiver, I check in my bag for something for breakfast, feeling totally ravenous. I settle on a chocolate bar and curl up in the corner near where the light's shining in to enjoy it. I wish I had my phone, not just to ring for help, but also for something to do. At this rate I'll die of boredom before anything else.

Looking around the bare room I wish there was something in here to occupy myself with. A book, or something. *Any* book. And that's saying something as I'm very choosy about what I read, usually.

After getting up and walking around the room a few times to try to warm up a bit, I sit down again and try to get some more sleep. It'll pass the time if nothing else. I try to imagine what everyone will be doing at home right now; Dad'll be having his breakfast, and Mum'll be fussing over him with the teapot, as usual.

It's Christmas Eve, so Dad's hoping to close the factory early, which means he'll try to get in as soon as he can to get everything organised. He's really particular about his work, and I know how much he loves it at that factory. I can't help thinking that guy with all the nose-hair was right about Dad yesterday; he *is* the clever one. Bob Robinson might have the title of General Manager but it's obviously clear to everyone that Dad's the brains behind the business. He's actually dug Bob out of several sticky occasions, according to Mum. Of course, Dad would never admit that.

After dozing on and off for a while, I'm woken by a noise. In my bleary-eyed state I have to figure out what it is at first, but then my heart lifts as I realise it's a car.

'Hello! I'm down here!' I start yelling at the top of my voice. Surely it's so quiet outside that someone's bound to hear me?

The window-thing's way too high for me to see outside, and I can't actually hear anyone, but I know they must be nearby because of the car. Where else would they go?

With a heavy thud in my stomach I realise there are several factories here they could be visiting. But that car—or whatever it was—definitely sounded close, and as Jupiter Jumpers is on such a large plot, I somehow feel they must have come here.

My stomach twists as I realise it might not even be someone who's looking for me. Maybe it's someone who's come to kill me? Is that the plan? No one would find my body, would they? Not for a long time, anyhow. Why would they? They'd have no reason to come here, if the factory's empty. Quickly, I shake my head. I can't afford to think like that. Besides, why would anyone want to kill *me*? I'm hardly a threat to anyone, am I? And, anyway, if they were going to do that surely they'd have done it yesterday before making their getaway in that helicopter.

On reflection, I think I need to take advantage of the fact that someone's here and start shouting again in the hope it's my knight in shining armour—or, at least a navy uniform and a panda car.

'Help!' I holler. 'Help! Can anyone hear me?'

No reply. I can't even hear it now, and I'm not sure if that means whoever it is has switched off the engine and got out to take a look around—hopefully for me— or they've just driven past. I suppose it could be a security company or something, just checking on the building.

'Hellooo! I'm down here! Can you hear me? Help!' I decide it can't hurt to keep trying; at least I'm doing *something*. I'm not sure how long I spend shouting, but when my throat starts hurting I realise it might be a waste of time and energy. After all, what if someone came even closer and I couldn't shout to them because I'd lost my voice shouting into the void?

When I finally concede that whoever it was has gone, I sit back down and try not to cry. 'It's no good getting upset,' I tell myself, aloud. 'What you need is a plan. Everyone will know by now that you're missing, so there's no way they won't be looking for you.'

My mind wanders back to everyone I love, and I imagine how worried they must be. Would they all be out looking for me, along with the police? I hope so, but can't help thinking that I'd heard somewhere that you're not officially missing until after 24 hours—or is that in America?

Mum and Dad might assume I've spent the night at the hotel, on Margaret's sofa, having been with Klaus all yesterday afternoon, whereas Klaus might just assume I'd changed my mind about going to see him—and delivering the key—and gone back home. Maybe no one has even noticed I'm not there!

It's the first time this has occurred to me, and it's a horrid feeling, to be fair. I think I want to cry again, but I'm determined not to. Misery only produces more misery, and right now that's the last thing I need.

It's mid-morning and the sun's shining quite brightly through the bars, leaving a stream of light that hits the floor just near to where I'm sitting. Dad wants to close the factory early today, so he'll be working hard, I should think, to get everything done in time. He really looks after the staff and I know he'll want to close as early as they possibly can.

Mum should be busy helping her WI friends with the food for the party this afternoon, and I'm sure everyone's rallying round to help get everything ready. I love the sense of camaraderie in Merryville, especially at Christmas. I'm so excited to be moving back there in the New Year, especially now that Klaus and I are getting so close—or, at least, I *hope* we are.

It's occurred to me that he might be really mad at

me for not turning up there with the key yesterday. The thought makes me reach for the hem of my coat just to check it's still there. How will they manage without it? Have they had to break down the door to get all the presents ready for the party? I really hope not, as it would cost a lot to have the door replaced, and would they be able to save the lock? The key's so pretty and I got the impression it was very special, so I'd hate to be the reason they couldn't use it anymore.

My stomach gurgles, reminding me it's lunch time, and I really wish I'd made those sandwiches Mum suggested yesterday. I never thought I'd say it, but I'm really longing for something savoury. The nearest I can get to it is having plain Digestives instead of chocolate ones, so I tuck in.

After that I entertain myself singing Christmas songs at the top of my voice. On one hand, it keeps me cheerful—sort of—and on the other, there's always a chance someone might hear me and come and rescue me before I run out of chocolate, which won't be too far into the future, believe me.

My umpteenth rendition of Merry Xmas Everybody is actually sounding quite good, now that my throat's sore, and, although I admire the sound, I can't help feeling sorry for Noddy Holder if that's what he had to do to get that deep croak in his voice. I stop for yet another drink of water when I hear a car's engine again, and quickly go over to where the now-dim light's shining through the bars.

The snow's starting to melt, sending a stream of water through the broken glass and down the wall, and I'm beginning to wonder if I'm more likely to drown than anything else now.

'Hey! Down here!' I try to yell, but it's not easy with this darn throat. I knew this would happen!

This time I can hear voices. It sounds like several people talking and tramping through the snow.

'I'm here!' I yell, but it doesn't come out half as loud as I'd have liked.

I'm on tenterhooks as I can hear them out there talking, but I can't make myself heard. Then I hear an engine again. Surely they're not going already? Did I miss my chance just because of my stupid—but rather impressive , even if I do say so myself—Noddy Holder impression?

My heart sings as I hear more voices. It wasn't them going; it was more people coming. Then another car draws up, followed by an even heavier-sounding vehicle.

I swallow more water before yelling again. 'Help! Help me, someone!'

Footsteps get close and I try to shout again, but my voice comes out as a hoarse whisper. Quickly sipping more water, I try again. 'Help!' It's no good, my voice has gone. The footsteps sound closer now, and then the light's blocked from the bars in my little window. Someone's here. Standing right outside..

'Help!' My voice is hardly there, but I keep trying.

Honestly, Noddy Holder's got a lot to answer for!

Looking around, I'm trying desperately to find something that might make a noise, but there's nothing. My clothes would be too muffled, and I'm not even wearing a belt that would have a metal buckle—just as well after all this chocolate, really, but not much help in the noise department—and there's nothing in my bag except some tissues and few bits of makeup. I pull out my lipstick and hurl it against the bars, hoping for some sort of impact, but it misses and just smashes on the floor. A rather expensive compact ends the same way, as does a pot of eye shadow.

Whoever was there has moved away, and it's getting dark already. I hear a car engine and realise they've given up. They don't think I'm here so they're going away. They won't bother to come back because they didn't find me. A mixture of anger, frustration and helplessness almost makes me cry, and I pick up a mince pie and hurl it at the window. If I was hoping it'd make a sound I was disappointed as it seemed to disappear. I didn't even hear it come crashing onto the floor, but I suppose it's hardly going to make a noise. I pick up another one and do the same thing, and then another.

At some point tonight, I'm likely to sit on a

squelchy mince pie in the dark, I just know it, but right now I don't care. It's all so unfair. The party will be in full swing now, and the children will probably think Santa's let them down this year. Everyone will be having fun and I'll be forgotten about. A tear trickles down my cheek and I wipe it away angrily with the back of my hand.

Suddenly, a shout makes me jump, and a light is shone through the bars. 'Chris! Chris are you there?' There's some kind of scuffling noise near the window, before someone yells again, 'Over here! She must be over here! Quick!'

20

'I FEEL A BIT SILLY FLASHING AT KLAUS, BUT HE SEEMS HAPPY WITH MY EFFORTS'

I hold my breath as a million thoughts whizz through my head. I daren't believe this is actually happening. I hear an engine and see lights. Could someone be manoeuvring a car so its headlights shine on the bars of that vent?

'Help!' My voice is very hoarse, but I think someone can hear me.

'Chris, are you in there?'

It's Klaus! He's here!

'Yes,' I try my hardest to reply, but my voice seems to have disappeared completely.

There's no way he can hear my whisper and I can't let him go off and leave me here, I just can't! I quickly look around, and find the last mince pie, which I was actually saving to eat later. I take aim and throw it towards the bars. I'm not sure where it lands, but I can take a wild guess.

'Ouch! Yep, she's definitely in there.'

Oops!

Although I can't see him, I can tell that he's right next to the bars now, as he blocks out the light. 'Chris, we're going to get you out, okay? The police are on their way and they'll break down the door if they have to, so we can get inside and get to you.'

Tears stream down my cheeks and I sniff loudly.

'Don't be upset. Honestly, they won't be long, and I'll wait here with you until they get to you, I promise.'

I can hear other voices in the background and then Klaus calls back to me.

'They're just arriving now, Chris. Don't be scared if you hear any loud bangs; they're just going to get you out. And stay away from the door in case it swings open, okay?'

I'm nodding, though I know he can't see me.

'Hang on a sec,' he calls down, and I hear him talking to someone else. 'I'm going to lower a torch down to you,' Klaus says. 'I'm not sure if you're tied up or not, but if you can reach it, flash it to let me know, okay?'

A minute later there's a torch on the end of a piece of string coming through the bars and down the wet wall beneath the window. I reach up and grab it as soon as I can and quickly switch it on.

'Yes!' he enthuses. 'Now, flash if you're on your own.'

I flash once.

'That's good.'

'Are you hurt? Flash if you're okay.'

I flash again

'Thank goodness.' The relief in his voice is palpable. *He really does care!*

'Are you in any danger down there? Flash if you're safe.'

Another flash.

I feel a bit silly flashing at Klaus, but he seems happy with my efforts.

'Are you tied up?'

I keep the torch switched off.

'No. That's good.'

Moments later I hear someone banging at the door behind me and I jump, rushing over to stand against the far wall, but being careful not to choose a damp patch. Unfortunately, in my haste I'd forgotten to switch the torch back on and in the darkness I've managed to tread on something soft and squidgy.

'Aah!' My scream actually makes itself heard as my foot slips from under me and I slide onto my backside.

'Chris! Are you okay?' Panic resounds in Klaus's voice.

'Yes!' My voice is still a whisper at normal pitch, it seems, so I quickly flash the torch once. I only leave it

off for a few seconds before turning it on again so I can
see where I'm putting my feet as I tentatively stand up,
clinging to the damp wall for dear life.

The hammering continues at the door, and after
one last-ditch effort it springs open and more torches
shine into my eyes. Two burly policemen step into the
room.

'It's okay, we've got you now,' one of them says,
gently but firmly.

I automatically reach for my bag before allowing
him to take my hand and lead me out of the little
room. The door's completely bashed in, and there's a
third man standing by with a battering ram in his
hands and a satisfied expression on his face.

'Are you hurt?' one of them asks, leading me
towards the lift.

*Well, my backside's just taken a bit of a bruising, but I
can hardly admit that.*

'No,' I whisper, shaking my head.

'Sore throat?' The other one asks kindly as we start
to rise.

I nod.

'You must have been shouting for quite a while,' he
replies with a sympathetic smile. 'Good job it paid off
in the end, though, eh?'

Actually, I'm not so sure it had anything to do with
my shouting—or my singing—but I don't tell him that.

'That boyfriend of yours is quite tenacious,' the

first policeman says, shaking his head. 'We'd already been out here looking for you three times, but he insisted on checking for himself. We were quite surprised to get a call from him saying you were here, after all.'

My stomach goes all fizzy and warm as I imagine Klaus putting his foot down. He really must care about me, and I feel bad for thinking otherwise. It's good to know that the police were actually here several times, too, although I must have been asleep some of the time as I didn't hear a thing.

'Be careful when we reach reception,' the guy with the battering ram tells me, as the lift slows down again. 'We had quite a hard time getting in the front entrance, so there's bits of metal and stuff all over the place. Some of it can be quite sharp.'

I see what he means when the doors open and I'm faced with what looks a bit like a bomb-site. They must have used some sort of laser cutting machinery, as some of the metal looks charred around the edges, as it litters the once-pristine foyer.

The double doors are wide open, allowing snow to drift inside, and there are a couple more policemen waiting outside.

'Take care here,' the first policeman tells me as he takes my arm and helps me through the mess and out the door. It takes a minute for my eyes to adjust from the interior lights of the building, to the scattered lighting of several cars, whose main beams are all aimed at the factory.

'Chris!' Klaus suddenly appears and comes running over to me. 'Chris, are you okay?' His warm arms envelope me in a tight squeeze and I run my fingers through his hair, which looks quite angelic backlit by the cars' headlights.

'Oh Chris, I'm so sorry for the way I treated you. I was just so worried—'

'The party!' I whisper hoarsely, suddenly remembering. 'Is it ruined?'

'No, of course not.' He chuckles.

'The key!' I reach for my hem and yank at the stitching, careful to place a hand underneath in case the tiny metal object gets lost in the snow—*I'm not stupid*. I hold it tightly in my hand before giving it to Klaus.

'I was such an idiot going on about it,' he says, and even in the light of the cars I could see his face turn a little red. 'I'm so sorry.'

His grandad suddenly appears behind him, beaming. 'I told him not to worry,' he says, shaking his head. 'I knew everything would be all right in the end.'

Klaus hands him the key. 'I should have known better than to doubt you, Grandad,' he says, rather sheepishly.

'I told you, it's a very special key,' his Grandad says, holding it up. 'Now, who needs a lift back?'

I turn to the policemen who are talking behind me.

'Can I take her to the party, officers?' Klaus asks, as though reading my thoughts.

One of them nods, smiling. 'Why, not? It's Christmas Eve.' He turns to me. 'We can't exactly expect a statement from you until you can talk anyway, can we?'

I grin at him.

'You know who did all this, I take it?'

'Drew Chapman,' I whisper. 'He had three other men.'

The policeman gives a satisfied nod. 'That'll be the guys we picked up at the airport. They're already being questioned. Hopefully, once they know we've found you they'll be a bit more loose-lipped.' He smiles kindly. 'We'll give you a couple of days to get your voice back, then we'll just need a statement from you, okay? We'll check on you, say, Boxing Day?'

I nod happily with a whispered 'thank you. Happy Christmas.'

'Happy Christmas,' he replies, beaming.

'Come on, your chariot awaits.' Klaus's grandad looks quite excited as he leads us over to his car.

'Your mum and dad will be thrilled to see you,' Klaus tells me as we climb inside. 'I phoned to let them know we'd found you.'

'Are they okay?' I whisper, suddenly worried sick about them.

'Yeah, of course. They've been in bits about you, of course,' Klaus replies as the car whizzes off out of the trading estate. He holds me tightly on the back seat. 'Mind you, they'd be even more worried if they knew Grandad was driving you home.' He rolls his eyebrows.

'I heard that,' his grandad calls from the front seat. 'There's nothing wrong with Comet, she'll get us there in one piece, don't you fret over that.' He shakes his head with a grin. 'And be careful what you say, young lad. I'm sure I've got some mince pies somewhere.'

Klaus bursts out laughing, rubbing his head. 'Yeah, what exactly was that all about?' he asks me.

I explain that I needed something to make a noise as I'd lost my voice. 'The mince pies were more out of frustration than anything else,' I admit, still whispering.

Klaus grins. 'They were a stroke of inspiration. As soon as I saw the iced mince pie on the ground I knew you had to be there. The one that hit my head just confirmed it.'

'Sorry, that was an accident.'

Klaus chuckles. 'I probably deserved it. I'm so sorry I was so stressed about the key; I wasn't all that kind to you.'

I'm not sure what to say, so I just cuddle him.

'The whole town's been out combing the area looking for you,' he goes on, after a few minutes. 'I was tracing your footsteps over to my place when I found this.' He pulls out my bracelet from his pocket and my heart leaps.

'The clasp had broken,' he says, 'but Grandad managed to replace it for you.' He carefully fastens it around my wrist. 'I knew something bad must have taken place for that to happen. That's when I called the police and insisted they start looking for you right away.'

'Thank you.' My heart's beating wildly. The memory of Drew Chapman hauling me into the car, the worry I'd put everyone through—I can't believe everyone was looking for me! I give a big sniff and Klaus pulls me as close as our seatbelts allow.

'Don't worry. Everything's going to be fine, now,' he promises, before kissing me on the forehead. 'They've just started the party and everyone can't wait to see you.'

'The party?' I whisper, frowning. 'They didn't start it?'

'No one was in the mood until we'd found you,' he assures me. 'When I called your mum to say you were safe and well, I also told her you'd be disappointed if you got back there and the party hadn't even started so she got onto it right away. It should be in full swing by the time we get there.'

'I'll take you to the hotel first,' his grandad promises. 'I'm sure you'll want to get cleaned up before you see everyone. Anya's waiting for you there.'

I can't get over how thoughtful he is.

'I'll head back to the workshop and get the presents loaded. Nick can come and pick you three up and take you to the party.' His grandad's clearly got it all worked out.

'Dad's over at the workshop sorting out the rest of the gifts,' Klaus informs me with a smile. 'He's been helping grandad a lot lately.'

'I can help you, too,' I offer.

'You already have.' His grandad holds up the little filigree key with a smile. 'Now the whole town will want to see that you're safe.'

My heart leaps at the thought of everyone being so concerned about me that they'd even postpone the Christmas party. I'd never felt so loved in my life! I close my eyes and listen to the soft hum of the engine, which sounds much quieter than I expected. It's a very smooth ride and I almost feel like I'm flying through the air, as we don't seem to have to stop, or slow down or anything all the way back.

WITH A JOLT, I open my eyes to find that we've arrived just outside the Hollies Hotel.

'Come on, Grandma's waiting for you,' Klaus offers me a smile, unclipping my seatbelt and extending a hand to help me out of the car.

As I try to shuffle elegantly across the seat, I become aware of something sticking me in place.

'I can't move,' I whisper, but he doesn't seem to hear me as he just holds my hand even tighter.

Why can't I get out of this seat? It's beautiful soft leather, very squishy and comfy, but I feel physically attached to the seat.

'Come on.' Klaus pulls me even tighter and I haul my backside from its resting place.

The 'glue' that seems intent on keeping me in place finally yields and I almost fly out of the car and into Klaus's waiting arms.

'What's up?' He frowns in puzzlement as I cling to him for fear of falling flat on my face. Then he looks behind me. 'What's that brown patch on the back seat?'

'A mince pie,' I whisper into his ear. 'Sorry, I must have—'

He chuckles, shaking his head. 'It'll wipe off.' He shrugs. 'Come on, let's get you cleaned up.'

Amazed at how casually he accepts my predicament, I smile and let him lead me up the steps to the hotel.

'See you soon,' his grandad calls cheerily before driving off.

I can't help wondering if he'll be quite so cheerful when he sees the mess on that back seat.

'There you are!' Klaus's grandma, Anya, is waiting

for us in the foyer when we arrive, and immediately throws her arms around me. 'We've all been so worried.'

'Me, too,' I admit.

'The hot water's on, so you can go and take a shower,' Margaret offers with a smile. 'Use room 101.'

'I'll bring up some clean clothes for you, shortly,' Anya promises. 'I'm sure you'll want to change for the party.'

'Thanks so much.' I smile at her gratefully, before Margaret leads me upstairs.

I hold my breath as I open the bedroom door, after all, no one knows what they'll find in room 101, do they? Luckily for me, it's a just a very comfortable-looking bed, a pretty dressing table and a doorway into the ensuite bathroom.

'There's fresh towels through there, and some washing things,' Margaret says, before leaving me to enjoy a lovely hot shower.

Tears of relief mingle with the frothy bubbles as I enjoy getting my hair and body clean again. It must have been filthy in that disused store room, but I hadn't noticed at the time. I'm just so glad I'm out of there.

It's lovely to clean my teeth and feel fresh again, and the hairdryer has my hair ready in no time.

There's a knock at the door and Anya appears holding something red on a hanger. 'Here you are, dear. I hope this fits you all right.'

I gape at the red velvet dress with matching, fur-trimmed cape.

'Klaus said you'd kindly offered to help with the presents,' she explains.

I smile at her, nodding. 'Of course.'

21

'WELL, I KNEW THE CAR HAD A LARGE CAPACITY BUT...'

'Don't you look lovely!' Klaus stands up and gives me a hug as soon as I arrive in the living room.

I feel lovely. I've even been given a pair of long black boots to wear, and a thermal vest to keep me warm—Anya's clearly thought of everything!

'Very nice.' Nick gives me a nod of approval, and Anya just winks at me.

'Thank you.' I smile, relieved that my voice seems to be coming back a little.

'Stanley and I will follow you there,' Margaret says, breezing into the room.

'Right. Let's get going, then.' Nick stands up and we all head out the door. It's lovely to see all the Christmas lights on in and around the hotel, and I stop and gape when we reach the front door.

'Wow!'

'I told you it would get one,' Nick whispers to me, as I gaze at the enormous, bright star shining down from the top of the tree by the entrance.

Nick drives us down to the middle of the town where the annual Christmas party is in full swing. Children are sitting at the large trestle tables, tucking into all the party food, and chatting excitedly, while several adults hover around them, passing plates of mince pies and sausage rolls round. Christmas music is blaring out of the large speakers that have been set up near the stage, and various entertainers are walking around the tables. I can see a clown making balloon animals to the delight of some of the children, and a magician pulling coins from behind a little boy's ears. A couple of very tall people—presumably on stilts—are wowing some others.

'Will your grandad get the presents here in time?' I whisper to Klaus, as I straighten up.

'Of course. We always do.' He smiles confidently, before climbing out of the car and offering me a hand.

'Chris!' Mum suddenly appears from behind us and throws her arms around me. 'I'm so glad you're okay. We've been worried sick. Come and have a mince pie.'

I'm not so sure I could face another one, but Mum insists.

'We won't be long,' Klaus calls over to me, as Mum

whisks me away to where a buffet table has been set up for the adults.

Everyone pats me on the back and cheers as I arrive, and I suddenly feel like a celebrity. It's all very surreal and makes me feel a little guilty, in a way. After all, I was never in any real danger, was I?

'Where's Dad?' I whisper to Mum, in between being congratulated on being freed.

'At the factory, love. Everyone stopped work to go and look for you. It wasn't until Klaus rang to say they'd found you safe and sound, that they all went back to work.'

I frown. 'But the orders?' I shiver.

'Klaus senior's offered to help out when he's given out all the gifts. Says he's got a plan to have it all done by midnight, which means all the contracts are fulfilled.'

'But how?'

Mum shrugs. 'I find it best not to ask about these things.' She smiles. 'Let's just leave it to the experts, shall we? Come on, some mulled wine'll warm you up a treat.' She leads me towards the marquee where the bar has already been set up.

There are more congratulations from the people already 'warming themselves up', and I feel touched by the genuine well-wishes of the whole town. I've never been so popular.

The mulled wine's delicious and really does warm

me right through. I hadn't realised how shivery I'd been feeling, and wonder if it's delayed shock, as well as the thick snow that's surrounding us, that's to blame. Klaus has lent me a spare coat, so I don't actually feel cold.

Mum can't seem to stop hugging me—she's not usually so demonstrative, but I'm certainly not complaining.

'Your dad was going to wait here for you—he honestly can't wait to see you—but I knew you'd be worried about those deliveries, so I told him to get back to work. I hope you don't mind, love?' She sounds quite concerned about my feelings.

'Of course not. It's not like anything really bad happened to me, is it?' I assure here with a smile. 'And I know how busy they are over at the factory. I can't believe everyone stopped work just to search for me.' I actually feel quite humbled by it.

'We were all at our wits' end, love,' she replies, wide-eyed. 'When Klaus said you hadn't turned up yesterday and hadn't answered your phone we knew something awful had happened. We were out all night looking for you, and then again today. Klaus told us about your bracelet and we all feared the worst.' Tears glisten across her eyes. 'Honestly, love, your Dad and I were beside ourselves. Klaus was very sweet, though, and never lost hope that you'd be okay. He was the one who kept our spirits up.'

'How did he know to check Jupiter Jumpers?' I ask, putting a hand on her arm. 'I was afraid no one would think to look there.'

'It was the first place he thought of,' she says, smiling, as she wipes her eyes. 'He said it was the only thing that made sense. You didn't have any enemies, and the one person who might not be happy with you was that Drew Chapman, especially after you two gathered all that evidence about their business.

'He told the police his suspicions and they went straight over to look for you, but came back empty-handed, several times. But they did start searching for Drew Chapman at the same time, and that's when they checked his phone records and found that he was planning to leave the country. They sealed off all the local airports, though they knew which one he was planning to use, and that's when they caught him and his mates. Klaus and his grandad hadn't believed that you weren't at the factory so they went to check for themselves. That's when they found you, thank goodness.' She gives me another tight squeeze and I feel so sorry for putting her and Dad through all this.

'I love you, Mum,' I tell her, my throat still quite hoarse.

She raises her eyebrows. We don't normally talk about things like that in our family. 'You too.' She smiles.

'Well, look who's here!' Frank and Fiona Poulson

suddenly appear behind me, and come over to give me a huge hug.

'Thank you so much for everything, Frank,' I say, as tears prick my eyes.

'Thank *you*. I might have lost my business *and* my best friend if you hadn't stepped in when you did. Some of my customers were most disappointed in those second-rate jumpers that guy tried to pass off as yours. I might have had a riot on my hands if we hadn't put it right when we did.'

I laugh, quite sure that Frank's exaggerating just a *little*.

'Fiona, it's so lovely to see you again.' Mum gives her friend a big squeeze.

Frank looks over the bar. 'Now, how about something to warm us all up while we have a good catch-up?'

A WHILE—AND SEVERAL 'WARMING' drinks—later, a loud popping sound entices us all out of the marquee and into the square where the firework display has just started.

The air is filled with the smell of sulphur and the sounds of 'oohs' and 'aahs' from both children and adults as we all marvel at the gorgeous colours and shapes in the sky.

'Lovely, aren't they?' A familiar voice mutters in my ear and I turn to see Klaus beaming at me.

'I was just wishing you were here,' I admit, whispering into his ear.

'I know.' He throws an arm around me and kisses me softly on the lips before we both admire the magnificent display.

When Santa arrives with his sacks full of presents, all the children squeal and rush over to him, excitedly. It's uncanny how authentic Klaus senior looks in the traditional costume, and he winks at me over the crowd.

'Let's get the rest of the presents from the car,' Klaus says, and we hurry over to grab a couple more sacks that are stuffed full of brightly-wrapped gifts from the boot.

'Comet's done really well having all this lot crammed into her,' I marvel, looking at the strange but beautiful large vehicle. It reminds me of a TARDIS with its capability to hold so much, and I momentarily consider asking Klaus senior to help me move all my stuff back from Greenchurch in a few weeks' time.

We take the sacks over to where Santa is sitting on a large chair, decorated to look like a throne with velvet and tinsel. He has a little boy on his lap, who's telling him how good he's been this year, and the old man looks like he's really taking in every word.

'Glad to see you making yourself useful.' I jump

around at the familiar voice and see Dad grinning at me, his arms immediately wrapping around me. 'Oh, love, I'm so glad to see you.' He loosens his grip a little to take a good look at me. 'Are you all right? Did they hurt you?'

'I'm fine, Dad. Honestly, I was just locked in a store room. They didn't lay a finger on me, I promise.'

Relief washes over my old man's face and my heart goes out to him.

'That's good. After Chapman was charged with attempted murder on our driver I was afraid...' He takes a deep breath, and I hug him all over again, wondering if maybe I was in danger, after all. After all, if Drew Chapman knew he was being charged for that, then he might have thought... I swallow hard, deciding not to think about it.

'I'm okay, Dad, I promise.'

'I'm so glad you're coming back home, love,' he murmurs in my ear.

'Me too, Dad.'

I'm fighting back tears when someone calls Dad's name, making us both look around.

'I thought it was you, Noel. And this must be your daughter, Christina?' A man in an expensive-looking suit is smiling at us. 'I'm Jonathan Hudson,' he says, reaching out a hand to Dad.

'We've spoken on the phone several times, but it's

lovely to actually meet you, sir,' Dad says, smiling as they shake hands. 'Yes, this is Chris.'

Jonathan shakes my hand too, much to my surprise.

'I've heard a lot about you, young lady,' he tells me, looking impressed.

I'm not used to that.

'You've saved our family's business and I can't thank you enough,' he goes on.

'It wasn't just me, it was...' I look around for Klaus, but he's disappeared.

'You were the instigator. And the one who put her life on the line, from what I've heard,' he insists.

Maybe Dad was right about that!

'I don't really want to talk shop here, but I just thought... as it's a celebration, and all...?' He looks a little pensive.

'It's no problem at all, sir,' Dad assures him.

Jonathan smiles. 'Well, I'll keep it brief, anyhow,' he promises. 'Now, I know Yasmine's already spoken to you about coming to work for us,' he says, looking at me.

My heart sinks and for a second I wonder if he's going to say she had no right in offering me a job and that he's retracting it. His expression makes me think otherwise, though.

'You're going to work in our advertising depart-ment,' he clarifies.

'Yes, sir. She's invited me to join the team.' I hold my breath, praying he's not about to sweep the rug from under me.

He nods. 'Not just *join* the team,' he says. 'We want you to *run* the team. Yasmine needs an assistant and we both think you'd be perfect. You'll be the assistant manager of the advertising department, if you're up for it, of course?'

I gape at him, wide-eyed. 'Yes, please,' I whisper, more from astonishment than my sore throat.

He smiles. 'That's good.' He turns to Dad. 'And, Noel, we were wondering if you'd be willing to take a position on the Board of Directors? I know all the rest are family, and we think it would be good to introduce someone from the factory to help make all the big decisions.'

I was expecting Dad's face to light up, but instead he looks at the ground for a minute before replying.

'I really appreciate the offer, and I think it's important to have someone on the Board who actually works at factory level, sir. But I love all the hands-on stuff, and being with everyone. It's been my life for some time now, and I'm not sure that working in an office all the time would really suit me.'

My jaw just about hits the ground. He's passing up the directorship?

'But, Dad...' I blurt out.

Jonathan puts his hand up to stop me, before

turning back to Dad. 'We thought you might say that.' He smiles. 'So, how about we give you the title of Managing Director? You manage the factory for us, in overall charge, and still sit on the Board? We could really use your expertise in planning the future of the company, and you've proven that you can manage the place even better than Bob Robinson. Heck, even our retailers have told us that. What do you say?'

Dad puts his hand out, smiling. 'I accept your offer. Thank you, sir.'

They shake hands again. 'Jonathan,' the boss says, chuckling, 'you're one of us now, Noel.'

Dad looks flabbergasted. 'I don't know what to say.'

'How about Happy Christmas? We'll talk in the New Year when I've got your contract all drawn up. And, by the way, I'm hoping to move back to the UK now that Great Aunt Stella's recovered, so I'll be seeing more of you and your lovely family.'

'You haven't met my wife, have you?' Dad says with a smile.

'Would that be the lady in the green coat speaking to *my* wife?' Jonathan says, nodding towards the buffet table where the two ladies seem embroiled in excited conversation.

Dad laughs. 'Well, it looks like I won't need to break the news to her.'

'I think my Mrs is as thrilled about all this as

yours,' Jonathan replies, chuckling. 'Merry Christmas, both of you.'

We watch him go, and give each other a tight squeeze, not quite believing what's just happened.

'This has to be the best Christmas ever,' I whisper to Dad.

'It certainly is, love.'

Jonathan Hudson goes over to where the two ladies are still chatting, and shakes Mum's hand.

Mum glances over at Dad with a huge smile. Suddenly both my parents look years younger.

'I'll go and rescue your Mum,' Dad says with a grin, and heads off.

'Actually, I think it might be Jonathan, who needs rescuing,' I say, giggling at the sight of the two exuberant ladies talking with him.

'Well, I think that's all the children happy,' Klaus suddenly appears behind me, smiling. 'Though I think Grandad gets even more joy out of all this than they do.'

'Mum said he's going to help with the factory's deliveries after this,' I remember, bursting to tell him all my news.

'Yeah, he'll have them all done in no time.' Klaus

leads me over to the marquee, his arm around me, making me feel all warm and gooey.

'Does he have a HGV licence, then?' I ask.

'He doesn't need one,' Klaus replies, matter-of-factly.

'But, how will he help with the deliveries? Dad's depending on him.' I frown.

'Don't worry. He'll manage.' Klaus glances over at Comet and then gives me a secretive smile.

Well, I knew the car had a large capacity but...

'Should we offer to help?' I ask.

'I've got a better idea,' he murmurs, sending delicious shivers through me.

We've reached the marquee, and I follow his gaze upwards. I gasp, noticing the large bunch of fresh mistletoe hanging above the doorway. I'd swear it wasn't there before.

Klaus is wearing one of his secretive smiles as we stand underneath it and he takes my lips in a lingering kiss that seems to last forever.

'Look,' he whispers when we finally free each others' mouths.

Glancing up into the night sky I see a shooting star zoom northwards. I smile, somehow knowing that his grandad has already left the party.

THE END

'LOVING CHRIS MOSS'
RELEASING IN DECEMBER 2022

BEA
STEVENS
Loving
Chris
Moss

MAY I ASK A FAVOUR?

I really hope you've enjoyed reading Saving Chris Moss, and if so, would you be so kind as to leave a review for me?

Bookbub:

https://www.bookbub.com/books/saving-chris-moss-a-festive-romantic-comedy-by-bea-stevens

Goodreads:

https://www.goodreads.com/book/show/59835894-saving-chris-moss

Thank you so much. xx

ACKNOWLEDGMENTS

I would like to acknowledge and thank all those friends and family who have helped and encouraged me to write this book.

My endless gratitude goes to my wonderful readers who enjoy and review my books and give me the incentive to keep doing what I love.

Thank you.

ABOUT THE AUTHOR

BEA STEVENS

Kicking cancer's butt, one step at a time

Author of Chick Lit, lover of chocolate (and doesn't think it's pure coincidence that the two sound similar!) Has a penchant for shoes, bags, clothes (the usual necessities), and socialising with friends, family and anyone else who gets dragged along.

Hopes you enjoy her books, get her humour, don't object to her use of British spellings and keep in touch!

Please feel free to sign up for her newsletter at: https://dl.bookfunnel.com/g5e0rhw7oh

And/or follow her on:

https://www.facebook.com/BeaStevensAuthor

https://www.instagram.com/beastevensauthor/

And check out her website at https://www.beastevens.com/

Get this **FREE BOOK** when you sign up for my newsletter

https://dl.bookfunnel.com/g5e0rhw7oh

ALSO BY BEA STEVENS

THE LIBERTY LAWRENCE SERIES

Twenty-something Liberty (Libby) Lawrence has a passion for fashion, a penchant for shoes and an uncanny knack of finding trouble!

Unlike her gorgeous boyfriend, Det Sgt James Harper, Libby doesn't have to go looking for crime—it usually finds her. The shop-loving pseudo sleuth has a totally different approach to solving mysteries, though, usually to the utter bewilderment of the hunky sergeant, who finds it hard to believe how heavily designer shoes seem to feature in her theories!

While strutting around in her Louboutins—usually putting her foot in it— Liberty puts her heart and 'sole' into everything she does. Life is never dull as Libby—often accompanied by Cassie, her best friend in the whole universe—puts the world to rights, one glamorous step at a time!

Best Foot Forward – The Liberty Lawrence Series Book One

RomCom/Chick Lit with a cosy mystery, a hint of romance,

lots of shoes, and loads of laughs!

Libby Lawrence has a love of designer shoes and a penchant for getting into trouble. When a thief strikes at her place of work, she's convinced the clue is in the shoes. The gorgeous cop who comes to investigate isn't so sure, and he and Libby become closer as the thief becomes more elusive.

Stepping It Up – The Liberty Lawrence Series Book Two

Liberty 'Libby' Lawrence is now working for the Daily Chronicle, though it's not as exciting as she'd hoped. She's running out of shoes to wear because she has to keep sprinting across town to chase stories, and her colleague, Dave, isn't as helpful as she'd like. In fact he's downright secretive.

James Harper seems distracted although he's reluctant to discuss what's on his mind.

Cassie and Rob are getting on great, which makes the situation with James feel even worse.

Libby decides it's time to think about stepping it up - in more ways than one!

If The Shoe Fits... - The Liberty Lawrence Series Book Three

Libby's exhilaration at getting her dream job is short-lived when she starts receiving threatening calls and, eventually gets kidnapped. Trapped in a burning building with just her wits and her boss to help her, should she really put all her faith in a shoe - even if it *is* a Louboutin?

Running In Heels – The Liberty Lawrence Series

<u>**Book Four**</u>

Never dismiss a lovely shoe just because you can't run in it – buy the shoe and walk instead!

Libby is really keen to move in with James—*honestly!*—but just can't tell her bestie, Cassie, that she's moving out.

James thinks he sees Libby kissing another man—but the reality is actually a lot more worrying!

And when Libby tries to help her friend, Fran, she puts herself in grave danger.

Will Libby ever convince James that she's not trying to keep things from him?

Can James persuade Libby to tell him when something's wrong?

And how can Libby *possibly* fit all her shoes into the tiny wardrobe in James' flat?

The Liberty Lawrence Series Book Five – Coming Soon!

<u>**Santa Claus and Puppy Paws – A Standalone Christmas Novella**</u>

Sleuthing in the snow can melt your heart

Signs that it might not be such a Happy Christmas after all:

•Getting home to an empty house so you're locked out in the snow;

• Someone burgling the neighbours;

• The police threatening to blow up all your worldly goods —including Mum's Belgian chocolates!

• Dad's first words to you are 'What've you been up to this time?'

Can Phoebe Fernlea turn things around in time for the big day? With the help of an injured little dog, a PC who's the spitting image of her favourite K-pop band member, and only a chocolate bar for dinner, she's certainly going to try.

One way or another, she's in for an unforgettable Christmas.

BEST FOOT FORWARD
The Liberty Lawrence Series Book One

Chapter 1

Single? *Single?* He couldn't even put 'it's complicated'? I suppose Facebook doesn't do a status for 'ended a perfectly good relationship to run off with a floozy East End barmaid with boobs like barrage balloons' does it? What's worse is that now *I* have to put 'single' on *my* page. Otherwise it looks like I'm either pining for him to come back like some hopeless wimp, or that *I'm* the one that split us up and flipping well cheated. I suppose I should be grateful he hasn't put himself down as being in a relationship with her—which is obviously the truth—but then I suppose everyone would know right away what a slimy scumbag he's being. And my *mum's* on Facebook!

'Miss? Are you serving?' An old woman's voice invades my thoughts, making me look up from my phone. I'd completely forgotten I was in the hotel restaurant.

She's a rather rotund, grey-haired old dear with pale blue eyes and a mouth that looks like it needs to smile more.

'Yes, of course.'

'I'd like the full English, please—but no tomato. I can't eat tomatoes. They give me the worst indigestion, you know. And make sure they poach the egg properly. I don't want it all congealed like yesterday.'

I drop my phone into the large pocket of my apron and pull out a notebook and pencil. In my head I also throw Connor Worthington into a large pocket—or a well, or a black hole, or the depths of hell maybe, which, I notice, must be where this old dear got the hideous gold necklace that looks like it's attacking her scrawny neck.

'Coming up.' I take the menu from her and plonk it on the dumbwaiter—which sounds a bit insulting of a perfectly nice piece of furniture, in my opinion—the hotel hasn't invested in the modern type with the mini-lift, yet. Then I make my way to the kitchen. I may be seething on the inside, but my outer smiley profes-sional strives to force her way to the fore.

'The grumpy cow in room 109 wants her usual,' I yell over to Justin, the breakfast cook. 'And she said don't congeal the eggs like yesterday.' Okay, maybe smiley didn't strive *that* hard.

'Flippin' cheek!' He sounds just like Gino D'Acampo—which is odd, considering he's from Croydon. I assume it's a 'chef' thing.

I throw him a sympathetic smile. 'Her words, not mine.'

'I never congeal *anything*. She should eat it faster, while it's still nice and soft. Congealed indeed!'

Justin's clearly ticked off and I just nod in agreement as I hoist myself onto the counter and idly swing my legs from side to side as pans clatter and bang all around me.

'Libby. A word.'

My heart sinks even further than it did when I checked Facebook earlier. My inner smiley retreats even further into the abyss. Mr Partington's frowning at me—again. I know he doesn't like me, but flipping Nora, couldn't he find someone else to pick on just this once? Doesn't he know what day it is? Boyfriendless Day 1 is what it is. You'd think he'd cut me some slack. Maybe even give me the day off to recover. Perhaps that's what he's about to say? *Libby, I read on Facebook that Connor's changed his status to single, which must mean you two have split up. I'm so sorry. It must be awful for you. How about taking the day off—or even a week? Go and take a holiday while you get over it. I'll pay you, of course. Double, in fact. You deserve that much, at least.*

'Liberty?'

Oh, no. He's using my full name. That doesn't

sound very sympathetic. Actually, he doesn't *look* very sympathetic either. In fact, he looks quite angry—he's red-faced and scowling at me impatiently. Behind his back we all call him 'Party', because of his name and partly because he's *anything but* the life and soul of the party. It's our ironic sense of humour. Which is something Party's totally lacking—a sense of humour, I mean.

I hop down from the side and walk over to him, my heart pumping like a steam engine. *I need this job*, I remind myself. *I really can't lose this job.*

'Come to my office.'

This can't be good.

'But the order—'

'Cheryl can take it.'

I give Cheryl, the kitchen porter, a nod of thanks, and she gives me a grimace of sympathy, eyeing the boss. *Yeah, thanks. I know.*

I wouldn't mind so much, but I'm not even a waitress. I'm only filling in while Fiona's got the flu. I'm actually junior management, though you'd never know it. General dogsbody, more like. Part of my job is to draw up the staff rotas but every time someone's absent I have to fill in for them. It becomes a juggling act with the rest of my admin duties as well as working in marketing and promotion. I'm in the middle of trying to organise the hotel's first wedding fair—if I can ever get around to it. This certainly isn't the job I thought I'd applied for.

I step into the manager's large, plush office and take a deep breath. It smells of lavender and polish. Or maybe lavender-scented polish. It's hard to tell. All I know is it's a damn site bigger and posher than the corner of the cupboard I've been assigned, behind the reception desk. It's actually a large, walk-in stationery store where they've squeezed a desk at one end for me to use. It wouldn't be so bad, but the admin staff aren't even that friendly. Even Frances, the white-haired receptionist wears a fixed smile and always seems gracious even when you know she doesn't really mean it. I secretly wonder if she's a robot. Anyway, I spend as little time back there as I can, to be honest, preferring to loiter in the restaurant and kitchen when I get the chance— there's a much nicer bunch of people working there.

My shoes, which clicked in an extremely professional, business-like manner across the tiled floor of the kitchen, now sink silently into the thick, cream carpet. *Cream.* In a food establishment? Well, food and beds, really. And booze—red wine, even. It's a hotel. A really nice hotel, I grant you, but still, there's a lot of stuff that can spill onto a cream carpet—as well as mud and... well, you know. *Other stuff.* Talking of which, I wonder about the dark spots dotted about the floor in here. They'll take some cleaning off.

Mr Partington's sitting on that luscious, swivel chair of his with the high back and thick, squidgy leather. I'd love to sit there. I once tried to sneak in when he wasn't around, just to sit in that chair. The door was locked, though. It's always locked. Even the housekeeping ladies have to borrow a key from reception when they need to hoover in here—it's the only room that won't open with a master key. I know, I've tried.

He leans forwards in his seat, looking wearily at me over his black-rimmed, Ted Baker glasses. I've seen some much nicer Gucci ones that would suit him better and I know he could afford them on his wages. Crikey, a general manager of a hotel this size, in London, he must be on at least—

'What did you think you were doing out there?' His voice is sharp and snappy—unlike his suit.

'Serving breakfast.' *What does he think I was doing— having a bath?*

'You do *know* that the door to the kitchen was still wide open when you shouted over to the chef about the order you were placing, don't you? I could hear what you called your customer from the other end of the restaurant.'

I frown. I didn't realise he was even *at* the other end of the restaurant. Has he been spying on me?

'And you know you shouldn't be on your mobile phone when you're working. I've told you about this before.' He's almost growling at me now. Yep, he was definitely spying on me.

'I wasn't actually *on* the phone,' I try to explain, 'I was checking something on—'

'It doesn't matter what you were doing.' His lips have gone all tight and his eyes have shrunk. 'You know the rules. You've been working here nearly two years now, Libby, and I'm sorry to tell you we're going to have to start looking at cutting back on staff. If I were you, I'd have a long, hard think about whether or not your future lies in the service industry at all. In the meantime, you *don't* insult customers, sit on the food surfaces in the kitchen, or use mobile phones in the restaurant. Is that clear?'

'Yes.'

'Yes, what?'

'Yes, it is.'

'Yes, it is what?'

'Yes, it is *clear.*' *What does he want—blood?*

'*Sir!*' he barks. 'Sir, or Mr Partington.'

I resist rolling my eyes—but only just. 'Sir.'

He huffs.

I stare at the floor. Those dark marks look almost like holes in the carpet. They leave a trail from the door, over to the filing cabinet, and from there across to the safe in the corner of the room. Hmm, I wonder if perhaps the boss has been carrying his coffee while he's been working and has dripped it across the floor. That'll take some shifting, dried in coffee.

'Just what were you thinking?' Mr Partington runs his hand through his grey hair with a sigh.

'White vinegar, sir. And soap.'

'What?' He'd look so much nicer if he'd stop frowning. Well, maybe not *that* much nicer. Polish and turds spring to mind—*lavender-scented* polish at that.

'Just mix it with some water and blot.'

'*What*?' He's frowning so hard I can't help wondering why he doesn't invest in some Botox.

'Coffee stains,' I explain—or at least, I *think* I'm explaining. He seems more confused than ever. It's a good tip, though. Beryl from housekeeping told me it when I had a little 'accident' in my room upstairs. That's one of the perks of living-in—you've got experts on hand for everything. Though you *do* have to keep the place tidy. And keep quiet. And you can't have visitors. Actually, I'm thinking I might move out soon.

Just then, Mr Partington's desk phone rings. He picks up, and I hear Frances telling him the painters and decorators are on the line. He waves me out of his office while he takes the call.

With a sigh, I leave the room, carefully closing the door behind me. He is certainly upset over something. And no one ever calls him 'sir'.

***

It's mid-morning when the bar staff arrive for the lunchtime shift, and I'm straightening up chairs in the restaurant, feeling more than ready for them. It's definitely a Spanx day—I could give Bridget Jones a run for her money any day of the week with the size of these knickers, and I'm even wearing Spanx tights to make my legs look thinner, too. My hair and make-up are immaculate, even if I do say so myself. They should be—I've spent enough time in the ladies' loo, preening myself. Cassie, my roommate and best friend in the whole world, gave me some of her expensive miracle-cream last night, once I'd finished bawling my eyes out, along with some designer make-up, and I'm really pleased with my new look.

I've got my hair in a smart, professional-looking chignon, with tendrils curling around my face, just to soften my look a little. We even re-dyed it last night, so it's blonder than ever, though not in an obviously fake way like Bianca's, just enough to lighten it a bit. I've done this smoky-eyes thing I saw in Cosmo, which has really made the blue stand out, and I've used one of those long-lasting lipsticks that doesn't come off when you have a cup of tea, or—God forbid—on your teeth. Connor's going to take one look at me and wonder what he ever saw in that skinny, long-legged Bianca Morrison-Wright. Apart from her money, of course— although, I did hear somewhere that her family's not as loaded as everyone assumes. Something to do with bad investments or something, I think. Oh, and her false boobs. You can't forget them. You can't *miss* them, either. But then, they're just that—false. Just like her eyelashes and her—

'Libby, have you finished laying up?' Mr Partington's really got it in for me today, and I wonder if he meant all that stuff about me not staying in the service industry. Surely, he can't actually mean I could lose my job? No, he probably thinks I should be doing more managerial tasks—like I'm supposed to do anyway—instead of filling in with the serving jobs every time someone's off sick. That's it! He's going to promote me to a more senior management position. That's what he meant, I'm sure of it.

I study his face hard, looking for signs of him telling me I'm about to be made assistant manager, but he's not giving anything away. In fact, it's quite disconcerting that he's spent so much time in the restaurant and kitchen this morning, watching *me*. Usually, he's holed away in that big, lavender-scented office, or having meetings with Mr Ainsworth, the Finance Manager, who's also the deputy manager and is on holiday at the moment.

I gasp as a thought occurs to me. Maybe, Mr Ainsworth *isn't* on holiday—maybe he's left. Perhaps that's why Party thinks I shouldn't be in the service industry but should be in accounts. I'm taking over as finance manager. There's just one problem—I'm hopeless with numbers. *Damn it!* But Gabby, one of the admins, is great at all that stuff and she's Mr Ainsworth's assistant. So, now she'll be *my* assistant. That would work—I can delegate all the difficult sums to her, and I'll do the important stuff like taking the money to the bank. Yes, I like the thought of that. There are several boutiques on the High Street I can visit while I'm there.

And here's another thought—I'll have a much bigger office. Mr Partington will have to show me around it and say things like 'Feel free to put in any knick-knacks you like, Libby. Make it feel like your second home.' I hope he's having it redecorated, too. A couple of the second-floor bedrooms are having a makeover—maybe he'll decide to have the whole hotel done. Something bright and cheerful instead of the corporate cream he seems to favour. I might even ask about hanging up some pictures.

I've just remembered he asked me a question and take a good look at the dining tables all set up for lunch. 'Yes, I think so.' Everything seems to be in place. In fact, I think it looks pretty brilliant considering it was all done by a non-waitress. 'Are you expecting someone special today?'

His face has turned red again—he's clearly fuming. Damn it. I forgot to say 'sir'. But I did *think* 'Mr Partington' so that should count, right? Okay, maybe not, judging by his scowl.

'Sir, is everything all right?' I'm trying to sound polite and concerned at the same time, but not sure if I'm actually pulling it off. It's hard to tell with him.

Just then, there's the click-clicking sound of someone walking behind the bar, and Mr Partington looks over. You can't actually see into the bar from here, but you can farther into the restaurant, as there's a hatch on the corner where the waiting-on staff place their drinks orders.

I recognise the sound of the ladies' heels on the tiled floor. Stiletto heels, I surmise. Size nine stiletto heels, at a guess. Nine, for goodness' sake. What's that all about? I mean, I know Bianca's tall, but *size nine shoes*? I'm dying to go and see what she's up to, but the boss cuts me off before I can move.

'There will be a staff meeting this afternoon at three o'clock in the Remington Suite,' he informs me, pouting. 'Pass the word around, will you?'

My jaw slackens as I gape at him. 'Today?'

He looks back at me, his eyebrows raised in surprise. 'Yes. Today.'

'Oh, *yesterday*. Damn that means I've missed it,' I say, thinking aloud. 'So why tell everyone now?'

'Not yesterday. *Today*.' He's frowning again. He often does that when he's talking to me.

I wish he'd make his mind up. 'But I have plans for—'

'Cancel them,' he says, his voice tight. He struts

across to the bar, presumably to spread the good news. Ha. My only consolation is that Bianca won't be happy. It's Tuesday and she always has her nails done on Tuesdays.

I hear her moaning and I snigger, heading for the kitchen. The staff there are as thrilled as I was to hear that we've got to stay back after our shift. I wonder if it would cheer them up if I told them I'm about to be promoted. But then, maybe the boss wants to tell everyone. Yeah—that'll be what the meeting's about. He's going to announce it to the whole staff today. Although... Party's not really one for surprises. Even when the hotel was awarded an extra star last year, he didn't make a big fuss. He just stuck a notice on the wall of the staff loos.

'We're only paid until three,' Margaret complains. 'Surely, they can't make us stay any longer than that? It must be against the rules.'

I stare at her. She's only been at the hotel for two weeks, and obviously has no idea how things work around here. I smile at her sympathetically. She'll learn. She's in her sixties with a shock of white hair— which isn't the only shock she's going to have today, if that comment's anything to go by.

There's a loud rustling sound and Cassie rushes through the kitchen's back door, laden with carrier bags. Her face is flushed with a mixture of exhaustion and excitement. Looks like she's been to Selfridges,

Harvey Nichols... oh, and I wonder what's in the little Dior bag. I can't wait to take a look later.

'I'll just put these away and I'll—' She stops short, clearly sensing the uneasy atmosphere. 'What? What's happened?'

Cassie's such a lovely friend and I really don't want to ruin her day, especially as she's only just got back. It's obvious she's had a great morning in town and will feel bad enough having to come to work as it is. She's on the late shift this week, working splits, and I know she had a busy time last night. Poor thing, she's the best waitress we've got and works like a slave for even less money than me. The first thing I'll do when I get my promotion is to give her a pay rise. Actually, she doesn't really need the money. That's not why she's here. But that's a secret only I know about. Maybe I'll keep the pay rise for myself and just promote her.

'We've got to attend a meeting at three.' Stan, the chef, only arrived a few minutes ago, too, and he tells her through gritted teeth about the impromptu meeting. 'I wish I'd asked Justin to do lunch now. Then he could've stayed instead.'

Justin's not as experienced as Stan, and usually only cooks breakfast and then sometimes comes back as a commis-chef in the evening when it's really busy.

Cassie looks crestfallen. 'Oh, no. I was hoping to try this lot on and take back anything that doesn't fit this afternoon. The fitting rooms were jammed, and I didn't have time to hang around.'

I feel sorry for her. The window of opportunity on a split isn't usually that big, and I know she won't have time to get to town and back before tonight's shift if she's kept in a boring meeting for an hour after the lunches have finished.

'Party's in a foul mood today,' I explain. 'He's been on my back all morning.' *But I think he's going to promote me*, I want to add. But I daren't. Maybe that's what's making him so cross? Perhaps he doesn't *want* to promote me. Could it be that I've been talent-spotted by someone from head office? A mystery shopper-type thing? I'm sure they have mystery hotel guests. They spotted me working and have given the order that I simply *must* be given a much higher rank than just junior management. Ah, now it makes sense.

Cassie grimaces. 'Something must have happened. I'll quickly take these up and—'

'You're late.'

Shit. I didn't notice the boss walking in behind me. He's glowering at my bestie who's turning a perfect shade of beetroot.

'I stopped her to explain about the meeting.' My hopes of placating him go straight out the window when the vein in his neck starts pulsating rapidly. It only does that when he's really mad.

'You need to see us all at three o' clock, I hear?'

Cassie's got that obstinate look in her eye. *Oh, double shit!* That look and his vein are a bad combination.

'That's right. Everyone must attend. It's very important,' Mr Partington says authoritatively.

'Even those of us who only get paid until three?' Crikey, Margaret really has no idea what she's doing, riling him like this. I cringe. The old dear's certainly got a death-wish!

His face is red with fury as his chest heaves and he stares at the older woman as though she's an alien. '*Everyone.*' He growls the word out from the back of his throat, and Margaret just gawps at him.

'I only asked,' she mutters as soon as he's left the room.

Everyone just smiles at her sympathetically, except Cassie, who disappears up the back stairs to our room with her shopping. It's the best part of living-in, getting to share a room with her. She's fab.

I retreat into the restaurant as the cooks start grumbling about how unfair it all is, though I know none of them would have the nerve to tell Party that to his face.

I fold a few napkins into swans while waiting for the first guests to arrive. My stomach is roiling with disappointment. Not only because of Connor—oh, no, I haven't forgotten about him—but also because I wanted to go into town later with Cassie. I've seen some Jimmy Choos online that would be perfect for a summer wedding. They're pale blue and have little flowers and hummingbirds on them. I've always promised myself a pair of Jimmy Choos. I can't actually afford them at the moment, but I'm saving up. I thought it would be good to check if they've got them in Selfridges and ask if I can try them on, just to see how they look.

Then I could start a whole collection of Jimmy Choos. And maybe some Manolo Blahniks and Diors —and, of course, my absolute favourites, some Louboutins. Though not those fake ones Bianca gets off the market—I'd have proper ones with red that stays on the sole, even in the rain.

Wouldn't they look great all lined up in my built-in wardrobe that I'm going to have when I can afford my own place, which might be sooner than I thought if this promotion comes with a decent pay rise. I've already got a pair of Stella McCartney red court shoes —or 'pumps' as they call them in America, which seems really odd to me as I always think of pumps as those gym shoes we used to wear at school with the sort of rubber tyre over the end. I bought them in a sale. I only wear them on really special occasions, of course, or, at least, I *will* wear them when I go to a special occasion. Nothing that special has cropped up yet since I bought them, but at least I'll be ready for it when it happens.

I've also got a pair of Kurt Geigers that I bought second-hand on eBay. They're a bit old but I wear them quite a lot as I still think they're really impressive. I'm getting some new ones just as soon as I can afford them.

'Shit!' Bianca's shriek hauls me from my shoe plans.

I was trying to forget she was there, although to be honest, she was one reason I was thinking about Jimmy Choos in the first place. I was so upset about her stealing Connor last night that I'd immersed myself in some online window-shopping to cheer myself up. That's when I decided to treat myself to a new designer wardrobe. Or, at least, start saving up for one.

Best Foot Forward – The Liberty Lawrence Series Book One

TRADEMARKS

The author acknowledges the use of the following trademarks in this book:

Chocolate Hobnobs: https://mcvities.co.uk/

Fox's Biscuits : https://www.foxs-biscuits.co.uk/

Digestive Biscuits: https://mcvities.co.uk/

Love Actually: StudioCanal; Working Title Films; DNA Films

Volvo: https://www.volvocars.com/uk

TARDIS : https://www.bbc.co.uk

Gucci: https://gucci.com

BBC : https://www.bbc.co.uk

Sherlock Holmes: https://conandoyleestate.com/

And the mention of the following famous people:
Albert Einstein

Noddy Holder
Mariah Carey
Michael Bublé
Kiera Knightly